There was this girl I knew called Sarah. For a while –
when I was younger – we hung out together almost all
the time. She was funny and happy and her voice went
croaky when she was excited. The things I most
remember about her are singing stupid songs that she'd
made up and threading daisy chains and lying on our
backs on a high, grassy hill talking about clouds. The
things I *want* to remember. We argued as well, though.
I don't want to remember her shouting at me, or the
time I told her I hated her and she cried, but I do. The
truth is that I loved her more than anything. But she
died before I ever really knew her: she was twenty-six.
She was my mother.

Rain's diary

6 July

Gemini: The solar eclipse in the creative part of your chart marks a turning point. This is a powerful day for starting a new project or making a new friendship. A meeting where your favourite food is served is lucky.

My dad thinks horoscopes are a load of rubbish. He'd like me to be sensible and scientific like he is. He works at a big drug company called Zoctine, and wears a kind of spacesuit all day to mix new formulas for anti-cancer drugs. When he comes home, his hair is mad and standing up as if he spent all day rubbing it with a balloon, his face is pink and sweaty, and he's too tired to talk. For an hour or so, he's too tired to do anything but watch football matches he recorded earlier. I got into football so we'd have something to talk about, but I'm never going to be sensible and scientific. I only like chemistry because you can sometimes make pretty colours in a Petri dish. I only like biology because the textbook has pictures of cats in it. I just flat out hate physics.

My mum was more like me. She read horoscopes and watched soap operas and believed in God. She never followed recipes properly and sometimes it really worked and other times she burned her cakes. She once gave my pet hamster mouth-to-mouth resuscitation (with a hankie between their mouths), while I looked on, too amazed to cry any more (although the thing was, she had accidentally sat on him, which was how he came to be quite flat and not breathing), and brought him back to life. I look like her, or anyway that's what people tell me.

My dad is still not beginning to get over her, so I try my best not to remind him of her when he's tired and home from work at the end of the day.

On Mondays he brings home an Indian takeaway and on Fridays a Chinese takeaway. Tuesday and Thursday, I cook one of the three things I can cook, which are risotto, pasta shells with mushrooms, and chicken Caesar salad. On Wednesdays, he cooks the one thing he can cook, which is shepherd's pie. Weekends are fend-for-yourself, which means on Saturday I usually have instant noodles and he usually has a whole six-pack of teacakes with nothing on them, and we make a giant full-fry-up for Sunday breakfast together. I love Sunday mornings. I love them so much that I spend almost all of them feeling really sad, because they'll be over so soon and it'll be a full week until the next one. Lately, I've even started getting that feeling of dread as early as Saturday. The fact is, when one of your parents has died, you don't take it for granted that the other one will be alive for as long as you need them.

But one of the good things about there only being two of you is that your dad treats you like an adult, because he has to talk normally to *someone*, and you're the only other person there. I'm closer to my dad than my friends are to their dads and, because he knows me, he trusts me. He trusts me to spend the occasional weekend alone, which is cool – 'cause I could be having wild parties where everyone gets drunk and wrecks the place, if I wanted. I'm not, of course. I get my best friend Georgina round whenever I can, because I hate being on my own, although I'd never tell Dad that. I talk a good game, but I get lonely, sometimes even a bit scared. And, by the way, I'm really worried about this summer.

Dad's going on a research trip with the Norwegian branch of Zoctine. He's wanted to do this for a long time, because that's where a lot of the research for the company is done, and my dad is a genius, really brilliant, and he could really make a difference. His boss has asked and asked him every single year . . . but he's always been responsible for me. So he's stayed at home while his colleagues (who aren't even as good as him) have gone instead. This year I convinced him that there was a better use for his experimental scientific mind than washing my favourite cream skirt with his dark blue towels and turning it grey.

It seemed like a great idea when we were planning it, and now I'm worried. I'm worried that Dad will be sad and lonely on his own without me, or will forget to stop working. This worries me for the long term even more, because soon I'll be going to uni and leaving him for longer, then even longer. I wish he'd find someone to live with, because I worry about him not taking care of himself, and about how often he'll eat six-packs of toasted teacakes and no proper food. Even then, another part of me is scared of him moving on, because it will change us both. I'm also a bit worried about going to London. I know what I'm doing here, I'm tough as a stray cat *here*. London might be tougher than me. There are muggers and terrorists and people selling heroin. There are tall skinny models and fashionistas walking around who laugh at people like me. There are streets to get lost in and buildings that are too tall to see over. Underground Tubes with a map that looks like my hair in the morning. And there's my gran. I haven't spent that much time with her before, certainly not alone, just her and me. What are we going to talk about every night? What if she doesn't like me?

I feel as though I'm always trying to think of the worst thing that could happen so that, the next time something bad happens to me, it'll hurt me less because I've been planning for it. But it just means I spend a lot of time being sad. Weirdly, though, this time around, all my worrying and trying to shock-proof the future isn't only making me sad. Behind the sad, trying to hide because it's a bit ashamed of itself, there's another feeling. I know what that feeling is, I remember it, even though I haven't felt it for a while: I'm *excited*.

PART ONE

Chapter 1

Rain was woken by shouting men. She saw the sash window, then the creepy china monkey on the mantelpiece and remembered she was at her gran's house. She shuffled to the window, tripping over her computer lead on the way. Making sure she couldn't be seen by anyone out there, she peered down at the street. She saw a traffic warden and a little fat man wearing shorts. Rain was on the third floor, but they seemed close. The fat man was slapping his hand on the bonnet of his car and kicking the air; the traffic warden stretched languidly against a wall and filled in a ticket, ignoring the fat man. The rest of the street was quite quiet and no one looked at them. In Rain's village, a little way outside Manchester, people looked when people shouted. The traffic warden tried to fit the ticket under the windscreen wiper of the fat man's car. The fat man tried to stop him. They struggled like six-year-old boys until the wiper broke off, and the fat man started shouting again.

Rain carefully ducked away from the window and sat on the bed. She knew she should go downstairs and talk to her gran but she was feeling a bit shy. The strange surroundings were disorientating her; she had to think hard to remember what day it was – Tuesday. She could feel the small ache of a new spot growing on her chin. But she was also hungry. So Rain pulled on a stripy towelling dressing gown over her baggy T-shirt and boys' shorts, tripped over her computer lead again, and went down the creaking stairs to the kitchen.

'Morning,' she said, pushing open the door.

There was a boy sitting at the table drinking a cup of tea and reading a newspaper.

'Whuah!' Rain shouted, jumping back.

The boy put down his tea cup.

'Are you okay?' he asked. 'I'm Harry.'

'You made me jump,' she said. 'I didn't expect to see you.' He had dark hair with a bit of a wave to it, and looked about nineteen. He was wearing a crumpled shirt, cords and heavy brown boots. He was gorgeous. Rain remembered she was wearing a ratty old dressing gown and boys' underwear. She pulled the dressing gown tighter.

'Who *are* you?'

'I'm Harry,' the boy said again.

'Where's my grandmother?' Rain said.

'Vivienne's in the garden,' he said, nodding towards the kitchen door. He picked up his cup again and asked, 'Did you want a cup of tea, Rain?'

'No. No thanks,' Rain said, and for some reason she was annoyed that he knew her name. She opened the door and leaned out, then stepped out.

'That grass is really wet,' Harry said. 'You shouldn't go out in those socks.'

Because he'd said *those* socks, Rain looked down at her feet. They were pink and yellow, with stripes running counter to the stripes on her dressing gown. She wasn't looking great. She tiptoed across the lawn to her gran, who was collecting sawn-off tree branches in a refuse sack.

'Who's that boy in there?' Rain asked. Her feet felt very cold and wet.

'Harry,' her gran said. 'Oh, Rain, I think you're getting a little pimple there.'

Rain put her hand to her chin. 'It doesn't matter!' she said. 'Who's Harry anyway?'

'He's helping me get the house fit to sell,' Rain's gran said. 'Get him to make you some tea, and then you can come out and help us.'

'I don't want tea,' Rain said softly, not meaning her granny to hear. She slipped back inside, tried to get past

Harry without him seeing her again – he didn't look up anyway – and went back up to her bedroom.

It had been six years since Rain had last seen her granny, and in that time, Vivienne seemed to have grown twenty years younger. Rain remembered her as an old woman at her mum's funeral – Vivienne's daughter's funeral – and then she'd gone away again. She'd been living in Germany with her second husband, and he had recently died at the end of a long, slow illness, and Vivienne had come back to London. The day before, Rain had looked out the train window as it pulled into Euston station, trying to find a little grey lady bundled in sorrow and sensible knitwear. Instead, she heard a strong voice call out her name, first loudly, then at speaking volume, and she realised she had been staring past her grandmother while standing almost next to her. And before she knew what was going on, Vivienne was taking Rain's bags off her and striding ahead to the taxi rank, while Rain hurried after her, silent and open-mouthed, taking in this energetic fifty-two-year-old woman with her sharply cut black trouser suit and black high heels with red soles.

Vivienne stopped at the end of the queue for taxis.

'Sorry to rush you, Rain, but we wanted to beat the suits.' She pointed behind them at the swarm of businessmen from the same train, lengthening the queue. 'Now, let me take a proper look at you.' She took a step back and Rain crumpled in embarrassment. 'You look like your mother,' her grandmother said. 'You're every bit as beautiful.' Vivienne closed her eyes a little too long for a blink. Rain felt a sudden stab at the back of her own eyes and blinked too many times.

They spent their first evening together asking a lot of questions but not really listening to the answers the other gave. Vivienne tried not to stare too hard at the young woman with her chin on her elbows on the kitchen table looking just like her mother had, tugging her fringe shyly like her mother used to, kicking her toes together the way her mother always did. Rain talked about her dad's work and the research project that took him out of the country this summer, but all she kept thinking was, 'God, my gran is *really posh*!'

Back in her bedroom on the third floor, Rain tried to look for her granny and the dark-haired boy through the window, but they were on the other side of the house. The third floor hadn't been rented out when her granny was in Germany – it held everything that was left of Vivienne's old life, all squashed into one tiny area: the house was tall but very thin. The shelves in every room were crammed with books, boxes, ornaments and papers. There were rolled up rugs and bags of shoes and old radios and clocks. Soon, these things would all be moved again, or thrown away, after her granny had sold this lovely, rickety house and moved somewhere smaller. Harry and her gran, she realised, were down there hacking through the wild forest of a back garden to make everything tame.

She had to get dressed. Rain showered and found her jeans and a stripy T-shirt, slapped on some make-up, felt embarrassed about putting make-up on just for Harry, wiped the lipstick off and went back outside. Her gran was at the far end of the garden, talking loudly to Harry: ' . . . the thing is, do I have to get planning permission for a bonfire in my own back garden?'

'Can I help with anything?' Rain asked. Harry looked over at Rain and she saw him smirk, then hide his smile before he went on cutting branches. She wanted to ask what he was smirking about. Maybe she wasn't dressed for gardening, but no one had told her to bring gardening clothes. Harry might have been gorgeous, but he was annoying, calling her by her name before they'd even met and smirking at her, and *making assumptions*.

'We could do with some more of these thick bin bags,' Vivienne called. 'Do you know how to get to the Portobello Road from here, Rain?'

'Not really,' Rain said. She didn't have a clue,

14

although she knew it was very near. She'd turned down Vivienne's offer the previous evening to show her around the area, and take a sightseeing trip this morning. She'd felt tired: it had been so long since she'd been here, she just wanted to take some time to get to know the house again to make a safe base before she started exploring.

'Harry, take her so she knows for the future,' Vivienne said. 'There's some cash on the kitchen table.'

'You take her,' Harry said. 'I can get more done than you and I've just had a break.'

'Not bloody likely,' Vivienne said. 'I'm not going anywhere looking like this.'

'Well, it's just that way, keep going all the way round the curve, second left after . . . ' Harry began, drawing diagrams in the air for Rain.

'Oh come on, just go with her!' Vivienne shouted. Vivienne had quite a set of lungs on her. 'If she gets lost we'll have to take time off to find her again.'

So Rain found herself walking past the super-expensive ice-cream coloured houses of Notting Hill. Her gran might have been posh, but there was no way she could have afforded to buy a house here now – millionaires lived in them. Rain's granddad had inherited the house more than thirty years ago, when the area was a lot grottier and cheaper. But still, the house was tatty now, knocked about by tenants, the garden overgrown after years with no one caring about it.

Rain had been here quite a lot when she was very young. She remembered one Christmas: her mum standing on a chair to put a fallen fairy back on the tree and her granddad whispering to Rain that she could eat the chocolate on its branches. She remembered a sunny day with everyone playing badminton in the garden, Rain swinging her own little pink racquet and always missing the shuttlecock. One autumn, racing her mum to stamp on crab apples on the pavement outside the house. Little pieces of memory. She went through them in her mind over and over again, not wanting to let a single one die from neglect.

'How long are you staying?' Harry asked as they walked. His cords were covered in dry mud and there were bits of leaf in his hair. Will people think this is my boyfriend, Rain wondered, this scruffy farmboy in the middle of a city? She crossly admitted to herself that she sort of hoped they would.

'All summer . . . until school starts again,' Rain said.

'Ah,' Harry said, 'and school gets serious next year, right? You'll be doing your GCSEs?'

Rain could feel herself redden with anger. 'A-levels,' she said.

'Oh right,' Harry said, pulling an exaggeratedly surprised face as he nodded. She wondered if he was making fun of her.

'What about you?' Rain said. 'I suppose you didn't bother with school past your GCSEs?'

Harry laughed out loud. 'No, I was foolish enough to keep going,' he said. 'I'm here at Imperial. That's how your grandmother found me, in fact: she put an ad up in my faculty building.'

'She advertised for a gardener at a university?'

He laughed again. 'You know Vivienne,' Harry said, and Rain thought, but didn't dare say, that she didn't at all. 'She wrote something witty and mysterious about needing an impoverished student who was prepared to do anything for money. I'm not just going to be doing the garden with her, we've got the whole house planned out. A paint job, bit of woodwork, getting rid of everything she doesn't need – we were talking about eBaying stuff off if we have time.'

'My gran knows about eBay?' Rain thought.

'Okay, here we are, London's famous Portobello Road, as seen in the film *Notting Hill*.' Harry held his hand out theatrically. She felt again that he was slightly making fun, or anyway making jokes that she was too unsophisticated to totally get.

The narrow street they came out on to was a crowded fruit and veg market. The pavements were incredibly narrow and passers-by spilled over the sides, waiting for gaps in the steady traffic of mothers pushing wide prams, old ladies in motorised wheelchairs, people walking their pushbikes. There were dozens of intriguing little clothes shops, trendy girls gazing dreamily out of café windows, people walking down the middle of the street eating hot oniony sausages in buns that smelled at once delicious and disgusting to Rain's hungry nostrils, a man sitting with his legs stretched out in front of him playing bongo drums, a little grey dog tied to a railing. Rain looked along as far as she could see, to stalls with teetering stacks of not-quite-familiar boxes of chocolate and, in the other direction, racks of dresses with batiky embellishment, and wacky shopping bags. She realised she'd lost Harry. She started to panic, not having paid any attention to the way they'd come. Then she felt a strong hand take hold of hers and pull her just a little bit too roughly forward through a group of young American tourists who'd come to a complete standstill, and she was relieved to discover the hand was Harry's, then annoyed again.

'Don't be hypnotised by the pretty trinkets!' he mocked, putting on a joky voice. 'And watch out for strange men. Young women have gone missing here and been found years later as imprisoned scullery maids for rich businessmen.'

Rain snatched her hand back from him. 'So where are these bin bags anyway? Why couldn't we just go to the supermarket?'

'It's not my job to question your grandmother,' Harry said.

They found the stall he wanted just in front of a branch of Tesco; it sold cleaning products, sponges, batteries, loo rolls and the bin bags Vivienne had sent them for, a pound a roll. While Harry bought four rolls, Rain looked enviously at a tiny, plump old man who walked past them eating chocolate brownies from a pink and white paper bag, pushing them quite steadily into his mouth as if chewing were not involved.

Harry, noticing this, asked, 'Are you craving a brownie?'

'Yeah!' Rain said, too hungry to act cool.

'But we can do better than those ones. Come on, down here.'

He led her to a road off the market street, and into an Italian delicatessen. Harry bought a paper bag of brownies and they set off home on a parallel road, this one less busy, eating the squidgiest, darkest, most delicious brownies Rain had ever tasted. She found herself warming to Harry, just a little bit.

Chapter 2

At seven o'clock, it was still as light as the middle of the day outside. Vivienne was downstairs cooking supper. She'd rented a DVD for them to watch, a scary thriller that Rain had wanted to see at the pictures, but hadn't been able to interest her friends in. Rain looked around her at the cluttered room with its time-capsule contents and tried to feel like a beautiful orphan in a Victorian novel. This was tricky, what with the late sun streaming through the window and Vivienne clattering around downstairs being boisterous and modern, occasionally shouting up things like, 'Do you eat squid, Rain?' (Rain had no idea. Squid didn't feature in her and her dad's never-changing meal rotation.)

There was a built-in wardrobe in the corner of the room that Rain had barely glanced at when she'd arrived the day before. She thought she should transfer the contents of her suitcase into it now, to stop everything getting creased and give herself more room. She tugged on its stiff door, and gasped when it jerked open. The cupboard was completely packed solid with stuff. So much stuff. More boxes, clothes, books, the same things that were in the room, but with *no space at all* between them anywhere. Rain ran downstairs to her granny.

'What *is* all that in my room? In the cupboard? Whose is it?'

She was hoping – praying – Vivienne would say some of it was her mum's. She was suddenly tingling all over and her heart was beating lumpily.

'Quite honestly I have no idea what's in there, it's been so long,' Vivienne said.

'Is any of it my mum's?' Rain said.

'Some of it must be,' Vivienne said. 'You're in her bedroom, or rather what was Sarah's bedroom till she was sixteen. But it'll be way back at the back, I bet. I just crammed everything in when I left the house. I don't think you'll find anything very wonderful, I'm afraid. I remember chucking a lot of her stuff out when she left home. You never think . . . ' Vivienne swallowed. 'You never think. Could you be bothered to make a start sifting through it, though? I know you're here to relax, but it would be a huge help.'

'I *love* going through old stuff,' Rain said. 'I just hope the summer is long enough.'

'We'll just make a few piles: chuck, keep, charity,' Vivienne said. 'It's going to take up the whole room, though. Why don't I move you down a floor to sleep? I only put you all the way up there so you'd have your own bathroom; there's another empty bedroom.'

'Oh, no, not if that's okay with you?' Rain said. 'I love being up there.' She was too embarrassed to say that she felt closer to her mum in the room, now she knew it had been hers.

'Whatever you like, lovey,' Vivienne said. 'We'll see how quickly the mess pushes you out – that cupboard goes back a *long* way. Now, how much heat can you take in your food? Personally I like it spicy enough to make my nose run . . . ' She held up a handful of tiny red chillis and Rain persuaded her to put most of them away for another day.

Back upstairs, after a little stumbling around, she managed to 'borrow' a neighbour's broadband connection on her laptop – Rain had been surprised that her gran didn't have an internet connection because everything about her was modern and ungrannyish. But then, Vivienne hadn't been back from Germany for very long. There was an email from Rain's dad asking her to call when she got the chance and talking about packing for his research trip. Rain took out her mobile and phoned him as she went through the junkmail, emails from all the sites she looked at most, some shopping ads.

'Hi, Rainy,' he said.

Rain wasn't expecting the tug of emotion she felt hearing his voice, which always sounded lower on the phone. She'd seen him yesterday morning, but it suddenly seemed to sink in that she wouldn't see her dad for weeks and weeks.

'You all set?' she said.

'They have shops there – if I forget anything.' Rain could hear him smiling. She smiled too.

'Yeah, I know.'

'Is everything okay there? You getting on okay?'

'Of course!' Rain said. 'Gran's lovely.' And even though it wasn't, not even a little, this felt like a lie because her dad's concern made her feel a bit sad and she didn't want him to hear it. 'She's making supper, it smells great.'

'Oh, you'll have to get her to teach you how to make new things!' her dad said.

'Yeah.'

They talked for a while, just repeating the last conversation they'd had at home. Rain didn't have anything new to say but didn't want to hang up. Vivienne called upstairs that the chilli would be ready in a couple of minutes, and Rain repeated it to her dad.

'Don't keep her waiting,' he said, but he didn't hang up. 'I wish I could have shown you round London,' Rain's dad said, breaking a short silence. 'It's where I had some of the best times of my life. Don't be afraid of it, but be careful.'

'I'm always careful.'

'I know.'

'Well, you be careful, too!' Rain said.

'I'll try.'

'Okay, then,' Rain said.

'I love you.'

'I love you, Dad.'

After hanging up, Rain went back to her email to remind her dad to pack his contact lens stuff, which he always forgot. Her best friend Georgina had written, too, and Rain skimmed it hurriedly.

From: georgygirl@globelink.com

Subject: How's it going?

Date: 19 July 5.17 p.m.

To: rain@zoctine.com

Haven't heard from you yet. Miss you already. Next week will be the first Rain-free party of the summer, Toni's seventeenth. Not necessarily rain-free – she's taking a chance and having it outside with barbecue. I think that's her parents' idea, to make themselves useful so they can stick around for fire-fighting and general supervision + no puke stains on the carpet. I'll be wearing your green silk top (thanks!) – but think it looks better on you. Still TOO

JEALOUS of you for being in London all holiday long especially as I will be in SCOTLAND with my 'other' family? And how are things with your granny?

'This is ready now, Rain,' Vivienne called upstairs.

'I'm coming right down, Gran, sorry!' Rain shouted back, but she finished a hasty reply, her fingers flying over the keys:

From:	rain@zoctine.com
Subject:	Re: How's it going?
Date:	19 July 7.19 p.m.
To:	georgygirl@globelink.com

MISS YOU TOO! Supper ready, rushing this, will write more later. Am gutted to be missing Toni's. Must get her a card or she will hate me – last year sent her an e-card and everyone knows that just means you've forgotten. Obviously there's nothing to be jealous about – I don't know anyone here, haven't done anything cool yet, and am VERY unlikely to go to any parties. But Gran is lovely, a bit insane. She's hired a totally fit student to paint/decorate/garden. Classic eye-candy, smouldering eyes, dark hair, dark skin . . . shame about the personality: thinks he's God's gift. Will watch him with his sleeves rolled up doing manly things, but avoid ruining effect with actual conversation. Can't wait to find out how Toni's party goes.

Rain knew she'd be missing the most important summer of their school lives, the last summer, a fact Georgina hadn't let her forget for a second as she made up her mind to come here. It made her feel scared all over, that she was giving up something so important, especially now that Georgy was no longer round the corner. But her dad needed the time off: if he was ever going to get on with his life, something had to shake their routine up. And now Rain had a project of her own.

That night, Rain dreamed that she was cleaning out the cupboard with her mum, who was talking to her about everything they found in there, saying weird things like 'This is my toy elephant, I call him Bill Smith; these are my talking dandelions, I carry them in my pockets.' When she woke up she felt as though she'd been given extra time with her mum, for free, and she felt fuzzy and happy all over. She looked at her watch and saw it was nearly ten o'clock – Rain hadn't meant to sleep so late, but she and her granny had stayed up quite late watching the film together. She stretched, pushed her hair out of her eyes, and went over to the cupboard. The wodged-in mess seemed even more intimidating than it had the night before. Rain took hold of a black bag and gave it a weedy tug. Nothing moved. She pulled harder, the mess seemed to lock together and edge forward in one lump, and Rain worried that if she kept pulling *everything* would move. She decided to go down and say good morning to her gran, and grab some toast and jam and milky coffee, for strength.

Bloody Harry was in the kitchen *again*, drinking his tea *again*. Rain was wearing horrible nightwear *again*.

'Oh,' Rain said, sarcastically. 'It always seems to be time for a tea break when I get up.'

Harry tilted his head on one side as he looked at her. 'I suppose you must always sleep exactly three hours later than the time I get here,' he said innocently.

'I've been making a start on clearing out the upstairs cupboards,' Rain said. 'I'm taking a break myself.' Harry glanced down at her pyjama bottoms, raising one eyebrow. She saw the glance and ignored it. 'Where's my granny?'

'I suppose you've been so busy with your clearing-out project that you haven't even seen her yet this morning,' Harry said, his eyes shiny with mischief. 'She's in the garden.' Rain didn't want to get her breakfast ready in front of Harry. She wished he'd finish his stupid tea and get a move on. She watched him pick up his cup again. 'Oh, let me get you some tea,' Harry said.

'You're not here to get me tea,' Rain said. 'Anyway, I really want coffee.'

'Whatever you like, Miss Rain,' Harry said, in an old-fashioned servant boy's voice, tugging at the floppy dark fringe that fell in front of his eyes. He chuckled as he got up to fill the kettle again. She was irritated beyond belief that he found her so amusing.

'Look, let me,' Rain said, but the only way she could stop him would be to actually take his hands away and she wasn't going to do that. So she gave in and went to make her toast instead, careful not to touch him as she squeezed past to get to the toaster. She glanced at him out of the corner of her eye as he spooned coffee into the cafetière, looking very at home. He was wearing jeans today and a thin black T-shirt that hung closely but loosely over his lean torso. When she'd made plans to come and stay with her gran, she hadn't expected also to be sharing the house with an aggravatingly pleased-with-himself, infuriatingly cute student.

She took her toast and coffee upstairs to get out of Harry's way. As soon as she'd closed the door behind her, she felt excited again about her mum's cupboard, and promised herself to go very slowly, and not miss a single thing.

Closest to the door were piles of medical books (her grandfather had been a doctor) – she carefully rebuilt the piles on the other side of the bedroom – then ordinary fiction books, then a massive stack of sheet music. Rain instantly flashed back to an old forgotten memory. There'd been a piano here when she was a little girl. Her mum had played and sung to her. What was the song she used to play? She hadn't thought about it in years. Silver something. 'Silver Begins.' Rain shivered. She felt like crying, but with happiness. Going further into the cupboard was like going back in time. The frail, spindly memories she had were becoming fleshier, noisier.

The next discovery was a pile of old records. Her mum had owned a lot of the titles on both vinyl and CD: tons of Madonna, some Prince, lots of old indie bands she barely knew, including a couple by a group called Lavender Sandcastles. Rain had heard of them – they'd had one or two famous singles, she thought, but she remembered her mum playing them when she was a kid. The group looked ridiculous – the male singer pouted with intense, mascara-ed eyes on the album sleeves – but vinyl covers were lovely to look at, they were so *big*.

One of the tracks was 'Silver Begins'.

Rain laid the records on one side of the fireplace and went back into the cupboard. She took out a big plastic telephone shaped like a grand piano, a mirror with a two-tone painting of James Dean running over the top of it, tangles of glass beaded necklaces and fringey jet hair accessories. A piggy bank that rattled with a lonely coin.

Rain's silent wish had been to surround herself with things that had belonged to her mother and revealed her personality, shared some of her secrets, to find *everything*, to *understand*. Now, on the edge of doing that, she was overwhelmed. She felt weak and tired. She felt she could never live long enough to read all the books, listen to all the records, and really know them, really live some of Sarah's life. She would never have a wardrobe big enough for all the clothes, or enough space for the strange little ornaments and possessions that were so painfully, truly, alive-ly Sarah's. Rain sat down in the dark cupboard with her legs crossed and cried.

Rain's diary

20 July

How long does it take for a face to go from streaky to normal again? Outside, my gran is doing gardeny things with a student called Harry – more about him later. Inside, I'm hiding in my room until it no longer looks as if I've been crying all morning. Harry is going to think I'm a complete freak, or a pampered princess, or both. This is my second full day here and I keep waking at ten and going downstairs to find him and gran up to their elbows in soil and worms, having spent the morning uprooting trees with their bare hands. Although why should I care what *he* thinks?

But I hope my gran doesn't think I'm lazy. I really love her in ways I'd never dreamed I would. She's funny; she tells hilarious stories about living in Germany and her ninety-year-old mother-in-law trying to fatten her up. She's so young-seeming – I know some of my friends' *mums* are as old as her, but she's not mum-like either. She's loud and bouncy and always rushing around and it hasn't felt uncomfortable being around her, the way I was afraid it might be. I *still* worry about us running out of things to say to each other! But I think the more time we spend together the more we'll have to talk about.

I miss Dad. I keep expecting him to be in the next room, I keep thinking I'll be able to talk to him later. All the same, it's good that I'm doing this alone. I've spent years always covering up my sadness about mum because I didn't want my dad to see.

But he can't see me now.

And I have more to cry about than ever; she's here. She's in everything. The mum I knew and the mum I didn't know, and I'm trying to knit the two together so I can come up with one person, the *real* her. I just wish I had a spare year to work this out and feel fine about it and then I could go back to my dad and I wouldn't have a streaky face and I wouldn't make him sad. To begin with I have to work on just going downstairs and seeming normal.

Harry is here all day long. He gets on really well with my gran, and she doesn't seem to notice or mind that he's a big-headed pretty-boy. He seems to be always making fun of me, which is driving me round the bend. My gran may be posh and live in a big house in a fancy area, but I'm not like that. And, you know, *she's* not like that! Her second husband left her with lots of debts and she's just come back to a life she left years ago and she's making her way through it completely alone and she's doing bloody well. Why do I care and why do I even think I know what Harry thinks? I only just met him. He has nice hair. He smirks too much. You know what? I don't like him.

Chapter 3

Although it wasn't a very big garden, Harry and Vivienne seemed to be producing endless bags of waste from it every single day. Rain often peeked out at them, watching Harry tearing at branches with his bare hands, and feeling guilty for not being any help to them. Still, she told herself she was also pretty busy doing reorganisation *inside* the house, and she hoped it wouldn't be totally unhelpful to her granny. Plus, Vivienne kept coming in with bits of twig in her hair, assuring Rain she wasn't needed in the garden, and they spent their evenings together, sampling more of Vivienne's experimental cookery and watching American medical dramas.

On Saturday, Vivienne knocked on Rain's door. The muffled reply seemed to come from next door. She knocked again and went in. There was no sign of Rain, the cupboard door was open and the floor was absolutely covered in junk.

'Rain?' Vivienne said.

'I'm in the cupboard,' Rain said. She backed out and smiled at her granny. Her dark brown hair was grey with dust, her cheeks were flushed. 'This probably looks a bit messy,' Rain said. 'But I promise there is a system!' She sneezed.

Vivienne was more amused than she let on.

'You've been doing this for *days*,' she said. 'You've barely been out. It's Saturday morning, it's summer and you're in a cupboard. Now, does that sound normal?'

'I know, Gran, but I started finding things and I couldn't stop. For instance!' She filled her arms with old clothes and held them up to her granny. 'My mum's! Look at this beautiful dress, it's retro-Seventies and . . . '

'Retro, is it? That's *my* dress, madam, and it's not retro, it's genuine old person's,' Vivienne laughed. 'I can see you're making progress, anyway. Do you have any bags you want me or Harry to take to the charity shop? Clear up a bit of space for you, so you can . . . carry on?'

Rain rubbed her nose with her sleeve. 'Well,' she said, 'I haven't really organised it as such *yet*.'

'Are you okay?' Vivienne asked. 'I think there are better things you could be doing here.' She took the top book off a pile of her daughter's old books and looked at it. On the back cover, Sarah had written her full name

– Sarah Devonshire – in the fat, balloon letters she and her best friend had spent a summer practising.

'Gran, I promise I will come and help you soon! I just thought if I sorted this out, all this stored stuff, that that would be helpful too, a little bit?'

'Rain, you didn't come to London to help me tidy my house or my garden or anything at all!' Vivienne said. 'I don't want you to be unhappy here, that's all.'

'Oh, Gran!' Rain said. 'I've never been happier.'

Vivienne understood perfectly; she longed to sit on the floor right now and start going through the pile of Sarah's things, holding her belongings. But it would be different for her; it would feel like intruding. She'd never have done it when Sarah was alive, and Vivienne respected her privacy now. She was also afraid of becoming too upset. For Vivienne, it wouldn't be about discovering who her daughter was, it would mean tumbling into the cracks of a heartache that she could still only just skate on.

'But you know,' Vivienne said, gently. She knelt down next to her granddaughter. 'You have all summer. I won't rush you or start throwing things away. It's time you saw a bit of London. It's quite a cool place.'

'No, I *do* want to go out more.' Rain looked apprehensive. 'It's just all a bit . . . And I know you're really busy just at the moment.'

'Well, all this is quite true,' Vivienne said, 'but

you're going with Harry this afternoon. I'm sending him to Goodge Street for a chainsaw.'

'A *chainsaw*?' Rain said. 'Well, why am I going with him? He's really going to love *me* tagging along, isn't he?'

'I don't think he'll find it that much of a chore,' Vivienne said. 'He needs a break, you need a break.'

'Well you need a break more than anyone,' Rain said. 'Why don't you and I —'

'I might be in pretty good shape but I can't carry a chainsaw around, and by the looks of things nor can you. Anyway, I can't leave Harry on his own, he'll dig up the wrong things,' Vivienne said, getting up.

'But why do I need to go with him?' Rain replied. 'And where is "Goodge" Street?' She said the name as if it was a weird foreign word. 'The thing is, I'm happier here and I know he'd be *much* happier if —'

'No excuses. Okay, I have to get back to my composting,' Vivienne said. 'It's sunny today, by the way . . . ' She was gone, the door clicking shut behind her. Rain wrapped her arms around her head and gave a little scream.

She had been making her way through a cardboard box of Sarah's schoolbooks when Vivienne had come in, and it didn't take long for Rain to lose herself in them again. Even the boring books were fascinating – her mother's careful little drawings of chemistry experiments made Rain just *love her so much*, the swirly style she wrote her name in on the front of each one, and the way for the first few pages of a new book her writing was so beautifully neat, then a few days later turned into a reckless scrawl. 'Would she have liked me,' Rain thought, 'if we'd met at school? Would we have been friends?' She imagined them both in school, checking each other out, or heading out in a group to the school disco. 'How,' Rain wondered, 'do people see me anyway? What am *I* like?'

She was thinking so hard that she barely noticed the books she'd been so fascinated by, moments before. Her head was almost *whirring*. But it was all forgotten in a second when she opened an orange exercise book with nothing written on the front cover, and read the first line inside:

This is going to be my first diary as a teenager: let's hope enough happens in my life to make it interesting.

Rain hadn't been expecting to find a diary, and she discovered there were more: actually a few *years* of entries in little exercise books. According to the dates written inside them, they covered her mum's life from the age of thirteen all the way to sixteen. Even before her head had time to get excited, her heart started beating like crazy. A hot and cold emotional rush swept through her. Was she the first person ever to read them? Rain leafed through one of them from the top corner, opening it just enough, her shaky fingertips slipping between the pages and enjoying the crinkliness, the little bumps pressed into the paper by her mum's biro. Every page was written on. Sarah's thoughts, her memories, answers to questions that Rain had been asking all her life, here, right now, in her hands. She took two deep breaths, uncrossed her legs, and started to read.

Sarah's diary

13 April

Just back from the youth club, which is always a bit of an event even though it should be the most boring place in the world. It's run by church people for one thing, and they only sell Penguins and Panda Cola. Tonight there was a big fight between Nicola and Joanne Ridley. It started because N was talking about J's friend Suzanne in the loo but J WAS ALSO IN THE LOO and heard it all. When it kicked off, there was a Madonna song playing, that smoochy one, but no one was slow-dancing. I was leaning against the wall wishing Paul would look over, just once, but I was also desperately not looking at him – but I'd still have seen if he'd looked, out the corner of my eye. Then I noticed everyone looking up and

Nic & Joanne were face to face on the stage, which you have to walk across to get to the dance floor. But what a place to fight. N knows loads of Fourth Years because until last week she was going out with Dan from the Fourth Year.

Rain stared at the paragraph she'd just read, and tried to go through it again, but it was sort of hard work. There were too many names to keep in her head and she was trying hard to remember them. It was just a story about lots of people she'd never know doing things that didn't even involve her mum. She just hadn't imagined her mum's secret diary would be quite this . . . *ordinary*. Were her own diaries as boring?

I'd heard it was Suzanne who split them up, but I haven't talked to Nic about it. Joanne told N it was no wonder Dan dumped her and everyone watching gasped. But N laughed and said she'd dumped Dan and she didn't care if Suzanne had her sloppy seconds. Joanna got really wound up and said it was her business if people slagged off her friends and Nic had better watch out! Then N put her hands on her hips and raised one eyebrow and said, 'Ooooh,' acting pretend-afraid. Some boys giggled. It was probably the COOLEST THING I HAVE EVER SEEN.

Rain unconsciously raised an eyebrow at this. 'Oh, Mum, it was not,' she whispered, smiling.

I was scared for her, though. It wasn't so long ago that Nicola was my best friend. I know she 'demoted' me when she started going out with boys and hung out with Karen more, but in a way that was the natural thing to do because Karen hangs out with boys more. I was still hoping she'd be okay. You don't mess with Fifth Years. But when the boys laughed, when she had the boys on her side, Nicola knew she'd won, everyone knew. I looked straight at Paul. He was smiling at Nicola and my heart hurt. I wish I was pretty.

Rain sighed. She wondered what Paul was like and if he'd ever looked at Sarah. Rain's dad was called Sam. Sarah had been thirteen when she wrote this. Right at this moment, she was older than her mum. Sarah seemed small and vulnerable and Rain wanted to protect her.

Vivienne brought Rain a sandwich at lunchtime and Rain swore she was almost done and she'd be down soon. She took a bite of the sandwich, realised she was *starving* and ate the whole thing in seconds.

Sarah's diary

2 May
Debs and I spent the day in Covent Garden, buying mad things at the Covent Garden General Store: groovy new pencil cases and stationery. We had lunch in the café there and eavesdropped on a couple of ACTORS at the next table

talking about auditioning for a film. We didn't recognise them, but they were still very glam, a boy and a girl, both gorgeous. When we got out to the cobbledy bit, we noticed a couple of lads looking at us and they started following us. Older than us, it was exciting but scary. We only managed to get rid of them at Miss Selfridge, where we spent an hour putting on tons of Kiss & Make-up stuff. Then we went back to Covent Garden, hoping we wouldn't see the lads again. And we didn't.

I love being there, though, you pick up on all the tourists' good vibes and start feeling like YOU'RE on holiday too. When the sun started to set, we noticed these big screens around the square, and they started showing an opera LIVE on them. It was playing at the Opera House, but inside, obviously, and they were broadcasting it outside, to everyone. I've never heard an opera before (and tend to run from the room when my dad starts playing classical music), but it was so amazing, being outside with all these people listening to that beautiful singing, for free, together. Oh, but we had to leave before the end to get home! Then we were messing around trying to sing the soprano's song while we were waiting for the Tube lift and when the doors opened there was a full lift of people gawping at us as if we were drunks or escaped lunatics, and we were crying with laughter all the way back.

Rain took the plate downstairs.

'Is Goodge Street anywhere near Covent Garden?'
she said.

Chapter 4

Rain sneaked a glance at Harry as they sat together on the front seat of the top deck of the 23 bus. She was trying to work out how annoyed he was that her gran had made him take her. Harry was looking down, trying to scratch a spot of dried mud from the knee of his jeans. She peeked at the long thick lashes over his eyelids, at his mouth, which was softer than the rest of his face, full lips curved into a slight smile, his bafflingly sexy neck. He looked up and caught her looking.

'Okay, so it makes sense for us to go to Covent Garden first,' he said, 'and we'll get the chainsaw last, because it's always better not to walk round town with a chainsaw.'

'I'm sorry you got dragged into taking me out,' Rain said. 'I'm totally fine on my own. We can split up and meet again in an hour or so and just *tell* Gran we hung out together.'

'What would I tell Vivienne if you got lost?' Harry said.

'I'm not going to get lost!' Rain said. 'This is ridiculous. *I* do not get lost, by the way.'

Harry turned away from her, smiling, and she could hear him humming a little tune as he looked out of the window. Then he leaned towards her, his shoulder pushing against hers, teasingly. She quite enjoyed the way he made her flop to the side every time he pushed, even though it was also, obviously, irritating. She leaned away from him.

'Why are you so anxious to get rid of me?' Harry asked. 'Are you meeting someone? A boy you met on the internet? Hmm, what would it be . . . a Harry Potter board?'

'Yeah, well, better Harry Potter than Harry . . . Flowerpotter!' Rain said, and immediately felt really stupid. Harry turned away again and laughed with his mouth closed; his shoulders jumped a little, twice. He didn't say anything, and they rode for a while in silence.

'No, I'm not meeting anyone,' Rain finally said. 'I just don't want to put you out and bore you.'

'I don't think that's likely to happen,' Harry said, then added, softly: 'I know you'd rather be on your own, but Vivienne probably has other ideas.'

'What do you mean?'

'Well, didn't you ask yourself why she sent us out

for the unique street-market bin bags at the furthest end of the market? How much did she save? Fifty pence?' Harry said.

'Huh?'

'I think she's afraid of you going anywhere on your own until you know the place better and she's using me as your personal Sherpa. I could have got a chainsaw closer to home, but she wants you to venture out a bit further today, I expect, start using the buses.'

Rain realised what he was saying. Oh God, he was having to look after her because her gran thought she was too afraid or too stupid to go out alone. 'Yeah, I kind of worked that out myself,' she said, sounding sulky to cover her embarrassment. 'I'm sorry you applied for a gardening job and ended up as a babysitter.'

'Don't make me feel bad,' Harry said. 'I think Vivienne doesn't really know how to handle you yet – she's a bit shy about taking you round a town she hasn't lived in for years, she has no idea where a teenager wants to go. And she knows I can handle you very easily.'

Rain flushed with anger at Harry's sly smile, but replied coolly, 'A teenager? WOW, are you really *twenty* years old? You'll let me know if I do something hopelessly immature, won't you?'

Harry glanced at her from under his thick

eyelashes, enjoying her sarcasm. The bus had reached Marble Arch, which she'd heard of, but she didn't really know what it was. It was a little bit puny. Rain had been to Paris on a school art trip, and they'd seen the Arc de Triomphe, which looked like this, but bigger and brighter and not just stuck on a traffic island.

They turned left and came to a halt. After about five minutes not moving, Rain said, 'What's going on? Why have we stopped?'

'You'll notice the fifty other buses directly in front of us? Our driver doesn't want to drive into the back of them,' Harry said.

'I can see that, but what's blocking them?'

'Other buses. This is fairly normal traffic.'

'There aren't even any cars!' Rain had never seen so many buses, two lanes of them on both sides of the road. But by now they had inched forward to the Selfridges windows, and they were amazing to look at – in the corner one, some good-looking real live people, not dummies, were lounging in a mocked-up trendy flat, eating lunch and ignoring the crowds that had gathered to stare at them through the glass – so Rain was quite happy waiting there.

Once they were off Oxford Street, the bus seemed to speed up a lot, whizzing past the gigantic Top Shop at Oxford Circus more quickly than Rain would have liked, and covering Regent Street in a couple of minutes. At the bottom was Piccadilly Circus – Rain was beginning to feel as if the bus route was organised to cover the whole Monopoly board. She couldn't help being excited by the video-screen billboards and the statue of Eros, which she'd seen hundreds of times in films and things, because it seemed to be the perfect centre of what she knew of London.

'I don't know why people go on those sightseeing buses,' Rain said. 'This one seems to be checking off everything.'

'But you don't get a charismatic tour guide on this one,' Harry said.

Rain flashed her prettiest smile at him. 'Tell me about that building over there,' she said. She pointed across Trafalgar Square, with its great big bronze lions, to a beautiful stone building with Greek columns along the front.

'It's the National Gallery,' Harry said.

Rain waited for him to go on. 'That's all you've got to say about it?'

Harry made a comic pretence of racking his brain for ideas. 'Look, those sightseeing buses are worth every penny,' he said. 'I can't compete with them. Although I could take you in there and they can't. So why are you starting with Covent Garden?'

Rain's mind went blank. Surely there was something there, some landmark that it was reasonable to want to see. She couldn't tell him she was dying to see the outside of the Opera House or ... what else was there?

'A friend of mine told me about this shop, the Covent Garden General Store?' Rain said.

Harry was looking out the window. 'This is our stop,' he said, throwing his arm across her to ring the bell, then standing up. 'I'm afraid I have some bad news for you,' he shouted over his shoulder as they went downstairs. Rain was almost thrown over by the bus's jerky braking; she swung wildly around the handrail she was gripping and her face thunked into Harry's hard back.

'Sorry,' she said. His T-shirt was thin and she felt the warmth of his body against her cheek. He gave her a half-smile and a look she couldn't work out.

'The General Store is no more,' he said. 'It's been a Marks and Spencer for years and years. I barely even remember it, but my big sister used to ... Who told you about it?'

Rain felt miserable and didn't want to answer him. 'You have a big sister?' she said, glad he'd given her a subject to change to.

'One big sister, two little sisters. Twins.'

'There's four of you?'

'Yep.'

'And you're the only boy? I suppose they all make

a fuss of you.' Rain guessed that this was the source of his confidence.

Harry laughed. 'They make my life hell, you mean. They steal my stuff and shout at me, then pretend they're sensitive little things because they watch trash on television and weep at all of it.' He stopped and held Rain's eyes with his own. She was looking almost weepy herself, although she was doing a good job of hiding behind her dark hair.

'The General Store,' he said, 'may be closed, but I can take you to places like that. It sold little gifty things and . . . '

'Well, it's not so much the *things* . . . ' She faded out, still not wanting to tell him about her mum.

'I know,' Harry said. They were walking into a tightening crowd of people, and Rain looked all around her and then quickly back at Harry to check he was still there.

'We want to be going up there,' he said, pointing ahead.

Some of the people were gathering around 'living statues': a man painted white pretending to be a robot and a motionless gold woman on a chair. There was a man playing a sort of horizontal electric harp, selling CDs of his music, and a quite old-looking punk with a very tall green Mohawk selling badges and iron-on patches that said things like, 'Once a punk, always a punk' and 'Pretty vacant forever'. Harry squeezed through in front of the crowds, where they'd left a small gap next to the statue people. Rain tried not to look at the statues, because she didn't want Harry to think she was some idiot from the middle of nowhere who found them amazing. But suddenly the robot man pointed at her, definitely her. There was no way for Rain and Harry to get through and they were momentarily stuck. She turned her head away from the robot, but she heard people around them laughing, and she felt nervous and looked back. He was jerkily getting off his plinth, still pointing at her, nodding now, clapping both hands on his heart. Rain felt herself blush all the way down to her chest. The robot was still making his way towards her.

'I think you have an admirer,' Harry said.

'Make him stop. Let's move, let's go!' Rain said. It was too late. The robot took Rain's hand and robotically lowered himself to one knee. The audience were laughing; Rain accepted her fate and smiled down at him. He sprang up and hugged her to him. 'This is assault,' Rain said over her shoulder to Harry. 'I am not enjoying myself.' Harry was covering his mouth with his hand, his eyebrows high above the dark brown eyes.

When the robot had let her go, Rain made a mad lunge towards the most spaced out part of the crowd and carried on walking. Now Harry was following her.

'Oh dear,' he said. 'How *embarrassing* for you.'

'Yes,' Rain said.

'But if you will flirt with robots . . .'

'FLIRT? I did *nothing* to encourage him!' Rain said, whirling around to face him. She saw Harry's laughing eyes, realised he was just making fun of her, and was too angry to speak. But her nerves and the relief that the robot experience was over were making her energetic, and she swept easily through the busy streets, determined to find some place to breathe. It all felt wrong: too many people, the sun too hot and bright, horrible mimes humiliating her. She stopped next to the Tube station and waited until Harry caught up with her.

Harry stopped beside Rain, opened his mouth as if he was going to say something, closed it and . . . just grinned. Then he said, 'Shall we go and get a drink?' He led her past fashion stores, boutiques, cafés, and finally into a pub.

'A pub?' Rain said, stupidly, and she couldn't help almost squeaking her surprise.

The pub was tiny and incredibly quiet. Rain couldn't believe the difference from the noisy crush of people outside. Her village pub was never this empty! There was only one person drinking there, a little old man with a copy of the *Racing Times* and a large, full pint of beer.

'A pint of orange juice and . . . ' Harry turned to Rain, who was raising an eyebrow at his unexpected choice.

'A Diet Coke, please,' she said, and her voice cracked because she was trying to speak quietly. Harry paid and pushed through a stained glass door into an even tinier room, the snug. He sat down on the padded bench and sipped his massive orange juice.

'You're pretty thirsty, eh?' Rain said. Harry's eyes narrowed in a smile over the rim of the glass. 'It's so calm in here.'

'Yeah, it's always empty at this time. It's a kind of secret hide-out from the tourist hell.'

'You make a habit of going to pubs in the middle of the day?' Rain said.

'It's the middle of the afternoon,' Harry said. 'But look around you. It's more relaxing than those coffee shops where you perch on stools drinking from giant paper cups next to giant windows. It has to be the right pub, though, and it's because we're here in Tourist World. I wouldn't have dragged you into somewhere dodgy.'

Rain glanced at him because he didn't seem to be making fun of her at all. She stretched her legs: she could feel herself unwinding in the soft light, the fierce sun filtered through the frosted glass. She felt embarrassed about dragging him to 'Tourist World', but also a bit irrationally hurt that that was how he thought of it. 'I *am* a tourist,' she said. 'But it's not really what I thought it'd be like, Covent Garden.'

Harry paused. 'It . . . changes. It's been a big place for shopping for a few years, but I imagine it's the sort of shopping you could get where you come from, probably.' His voice was gentle. 'And you're not a tourist: this summer you're a Londoner. Was there something else you wanted to see here?'

Rain smiled, a little sadly. 'To be honest, I didn't have a plan. I don't know where I want to go. We may as well just go for the chainsaw straight away.'

'We can just wander,' Harry said. 'Shall we buy Vivienne something? As proof that we're out and about?'

'Oh, that's a great idea,' Rain said. 'But I . . . The thing is, I don't know how much Gran's told you, but we haven't really seen much of each other for years. I'm not even sure I'd know what she liked.'

'Well, I wasn't hoping to fulfil her heart's desire,' Harry said. 'I was just thinking something to make her laugh?'

'Oh, right.' Rain mashed up the lemon slice in her Coke with the straw, then sucked up the pulpy drink, trying to think of what to say next. It was as if in a single moment the way they were together had changed, and she'd gone from being a kid Harry was

53

babysitting to a girl on a date. Not that she thought Harry had romance on his mind. It was more like realising she was alone with this boy and had to *talk* to him rather than just swat away his teasing.

She was just about to speak when Harry said, 'I suppose it's been hard for her to come back to this house when she has so many memories here.'

'Yes,' Rain said. She was surprised he'd said that – Vivienne was so loud and breezy all the time, it didn't occur to Rain that anyone might see a more vulnerable side.

'Your mum was very young when she died, wasn't she?'

Rain stared at him. People didn't normally talk to her about her mum, and she was self-conscious about making people uncomfortable if she tried to, so she didn't often try. Harry stared right back; his dark eyes were unfathomable, but so soft.

'Twenty-six,' Rain said huskily. 'She was twenty-six.'

'How old were you?'

'I was ten.'

'Then you had a *little* bit of time to get to know her,' Harry said. 'That's good, I mean it's something. Anything, I mean, is something.' Rain nodded silently. 'She was only sixteen when you were born?'

'She was younger than I am now,' Rain said. 'I can't

really get my head round it. My dad was nineteen. They got married straight away, before I was born.'

'This is the first time you've been to Vivienne's house without her?'

'Yes.'

'*She* told you about Covent Garden?'

'Sort of,' Rain said. 'I found . . . I read her diary. Do you think that's wrong?' Rain looked at her fingers as she asked the question. One of her nails was broken deep into the bed. She pulled it across, drawing blood.

'Of course it's not wrong,' Harry said. 'Look whatever you . . .' The barmaid came in and took away Rain's empty glass, then went out again. Harry sighed quietly and turned over her empty beer mat, then took a sip of his orange. 'Would you like another drink?' he said. Rain shook her head. Harry flipped the beer mat again. 'I had a brother. Who died.' He wasn't looking at her now. 'He was older than me. He died when I was five. I was too young to remember much about him, but I still feel . . . like he should be there, or will be again, I feel that a lot. Isn't that crazy?'

'No,' Rain whispered.

'And I . . . sometimes I look at pictures taken of both of us and think I can remember what happened when they were taken and the day around them, but why would I remember those days better? Which means I'm probably making it up.'

'No, I do that. It's that you started remembering those days closer to when they happened, because you've seen the pictures all your life. The memories aren't made up.'

Harry stretched, arching backwards so his ribs stood out. 'Sorry, Rain, I didn't mean to get you down.'

'You haven't,' Rain said, looking at him with a half-smile.

'Listen, we should probably make a move,' he said, adding in a lighter voice, 'I've got some ideas for Vivienne's present – I think we should head back through the market.'

Rain glanced anxiously at Harry. 'I'm just not sure we'll find the kind of thing that's right for my granny there,' she said, fiddling with a beer mat.

'Oh, of course, I see what you're saying,' Harry said. 'Don't worry, I promise to I'll protect you from the evil robot.' Rain glared at him.

On their way out, Harry and Rain had to come back through the main room of the pub. To Rain's horror the robot man was sitting there at one of the tables, sprawled lazily on a green leather banquette, sipping a tall, golden pint of beer, his other hand deep in a bag of pork scratchings. He made a jerky robot salute to her with the porky hand. Rain dived for the door, rushing through it with Harry's deep, noisy laugh chasing her.

She didn't turn round and let him see her smile.

Back outside, the street seemed even noisier and busier after the hush of the pub. But now Rain felt relaxed and ready for it, and, in turn, the packed streets seemed livelier, less scorched by the sun. They stopped at the ageing punk's stall to buy her grandmother a 'Once a punk always a punk' iron-on badge – Harry said he'd noticed her gardening trousers had holes in the knees. In the tourist crowd around them, Rain now saw groups of girls the same age as her, dressed up and laughing, looking pretty – Japanese girls with knee socks and candy-coloured kitten-heels, tall Scandinavian blondes in jeans and knotted shirts showing flat brown tummies. She heard northern accents like her own, and a busker with an electric guitar and portable amp playing cheesy old rock songs. Not exactly opera – Aerosmith instead of arias – but as Rain and her new friend wove through the tourists together, it was a good enough soundtrack.

Rain's diary

23 July

It's what they say at funerals, the thing that Harry said. Anything is something, any time you got to spend with the person you loved. You have to celebrate the fact that you knew them even at all before they died and be happy about the time you spent with them. It's what they said at her funeral, all the tall grown-ups who came up to talk to me after spending all afternoon staring at me. At the time, it made me so angry I could have screamed, but I was holding back my tears so hard my voice didn't work. Maybe they said it to Harry too. Maybe he believed them.

I didn't believe them because I knew it wasn't supposed to happen that way. When she died I thought mothers only died in fairy tales – where they die *so easily* that it never felt as though anything very bad at all had happened; it was the thing that made their stories begin. When it happened to me, I knew I wouldn't get wishes and fairy Godmothers and princes to help ease the pain, just a hole in my heart that got bigger and blacker until it sometimes felt like all of me was crumbling into it.

I couldn't be happy that I'd known her for ten years – for at least half of which I hadn't been paying attention. At the very least I wanted to have my ten years at a time when it was more convenient, when I'd use the time properly and count my blessings and be grateful and *know.* Know what was coming. Know it wouldn't last.

But when I talked to Harry today I almost saw it. Maybe because of what happened to him: I knew he knew what he was talking about. Maybe it was just because I never talk about her at all, usually.

But it made me feel . . . *just for that moment* . . .

Less sad.

Chapter 5

From: s.lindsay@zoctine.com

Subject: Variant mass

Date: 27 July 2.51 a.m.

To: rain@zoctine.com

Rainy, hi. How's my girl? It feels like a year since I saw you, and it's barely more than a week. I feel bad that I'm living here in the most astonishing natural beauty while I've sent you to live in our polluted capital. Norway is stunning. We're surrounded by black craggy mountains and the waterfalls are explosive and Godly. It's like – oh, you're better with words than me! – it's like everything isn't real, just giant ornaments in a kind of Martian Paradise. It's magical – the air so clean that breathing it in is making me years younger. And the weirdest thing is that it's always daytime, or something like daytime, or nothing like daytime. The sun barely sets before it rises again, it lingers in the crystal skies while you blink and blink and wait for night that never comes, then the sunrise is lighter, more brilliant, impossibly lovely colours. I'm writing this at 2.30 a.m. because I stayed up to watch the sunset/sunrise and can't tear myself from the show. Next time I come, I'm bringing you!

You've asked me three times if I'm eating properly so I may as well tell you the ugly truth. The answer is yes. But I'm eating out so much – I seem to have a lunch with colleagues and/or a formal dinner every day – that by the time we see each other again, I'll be an unrecognisable bona fide porker. Big fat Dad. And no, I haven't had my hair cut yet, I haven't had time and I don't know where to go. You know I really like the way Carlo does it at A Cut Above. It may not be fashionable, but it gives me exactly the right amount of fluff over the ears, which is important to a man.

Yes, I am enjoying myself – enjoying isn't the word – and you were right to make me come. And yes, you are always right! You would find us all unbelievably boring, but it is doing me good meeting lots of scientists. There's a lot of jokes about density over breakfast. (The breakfasts are pretty gigantic too.)

I'm glad you're getting on with Vivienne. Personally I've always been a bit scared of her, but men should be scared of their mothers-in-law.

It's strange for me spending so much time without

61

you, and to be experiencing this beauty without my favourite person in the world. I miss you very much, Rainy.

Love Dad

Rain smiled with real pleasure, thinking of her skinny father with his slightly wild hair and bright, brilliant eyes, gasping with pleasure at his strange sunrise. Her own eyes filled with happy tears.

Georgina's email was still downloading because it had so many attachments – seven photos.

From:	georgygirl@globelink.com
Subject:	Holy Moley it's Toni's Birthday!
Date:	27 July 8.55 a.m.
To:	rain@zoctine.com

I look drunk in all these pictures, but I wasn't. I just blink a lot. A photographer once told me I would never look good in pictures because I have a slow, frequent blink. Anyway! Here, here and here am I in your green silk top and towards the end of this photo story you'll see the other person who got inside your green silk top that night! (BUT THAT WAS ALL!) Rain Rain Rainy Rain, I got off with James Stephanos! Do you forgive me? Do you think he pretended it was you? Seriously, are you okay with this? Email me back immediately.

James Stephanos had been Rain's very first boyfriend, for two weeks back in Year Eight. But she'd had a crush on him for two years before that, so really it had been more serious than it sounded. The relationship, when it happened (and set up by none other than Georgina), had been a disaster, with neither of them having anything to say on the three dates they went on, and Rain eventually trying to avoid him in school. It ended politely and with no heartbreak on either side – just an easy, straightforward mistake, like getting a pair of shoes home, realising you would never wear them, and taking them back the next Saturday. And Rain laughed out loud when she read Georgy's email . . . but, as she was looking carefully at all the pictures, she did feel quite sad about Georgy and James kissing. It made her feel forgotten.

From:	rain@zoctine.com
Subject:	We can never be friends again
Date:	27 July 9.22 a.m.
To:	georgygirl@globelink.com

Kidding. James got further with you than he ever did with me, you tart!

Was it a drunken mistake or do you like him? Why didn't I know anything about this before? Or was there some moment at the party where everything changed?

You can't leave me dangling like this! I'm going to press send, and then I'm going to phone you! So expect a call before you even READ this! Here I come!

Rain leaned back from her computer and sucked her lips. Everyone was getting on very well without her. Her dad was eating proper breakfasts, Georgy was eating James's tongue. It was all good. It was what she'd have hoped would happen. So why did it make her feel lonely? Or was she just missing them? She found her phone, raked back her hair with her fingers, pulled herself together, and called Georgina.

'All right, you vixen, tell me what happened,' Rain said.

'Seriously, Rainy, are you okay with it?'

'I've had two boyfriends since James, what are you talking about?' Her voice squeaked, as if Georgy was totally crazy.

'I know that, and I wasn't *seriously* worried because if I'd been *seriously* worried I'd have left him alone. I just want to be sure. It's WEIRD you not being here. It's WEIRD going to things without you.'

'It might be WEIRD for you, it's torture for me. What have I missed? Who else got off with who?'

Georgina talked and talked and Rain listened and laughed. She loved more than almost everything in the world the way her best friend told stories, including every detail, remembering every word of every conversation, and tantalisingly focusing on something apparently unrelated and trivial that would be important later. She SHOUTED when she got excited. It was almost worth missing things to have Georgy get her up to speed.

Georgy eventually remembered to take a breath. 'All right, your turn,' she said. 'Tell me everything you've been doing.'

Rain felt a little rush of panic as she decided whether or not to lie. 'Well, I'm in a really nice part of town, the weather's been . . . oh, Georgy, the fact is I've spent most of the time in a cupboard.'

'What do you mean, a CUPBOARD?' Georgy said. 'What about the gorgeous handyman-type boy?'

'Oh!' Rain said, blushing suddenly as she thought of Harry and the way she'd first described him to her friend. 'We sort of had a moment. I mean, we're friends now. *Just* friends.'

'JUST friends? What's this moment? The cupboard action didn't involve him, then?'

Rain explained how the cupboard action had not been at all romantic. Georgy listened, her impatient interruptions coming less often, her voice softening. 'Oh, sweetie. But you're in London and you've been there more than a WEEK. You have to get out and see things. At least go shopping! Do it for me! You know

I'd swap places with you in a second.'

'If only you could come down,' Rain said.

'And you know I've got this majorly tedious family holiday in a few days and I can't come and see you for at least a month, if at all. Oh, WHY do my parents have to go away for three weeks anyway? People go to ANTIGUA for three weeks, not to the middle of nowhere. I know my dad loves hanging out with his sister and it's sort of fun, sometimes, with everyone there, but it's still probably illegal to make people stay so far away from the internet for that long. My sister and our airhead cousins will drive everyone INSANE because they're bringing their karaoke machine, we'll all have run out of things to say to each other by the end of the first week, it's STUPID and it's SCOTLAND, it won't even be WARM! Oh, anyway, there's nothing I can do.'

'Yeah . . . ' Rain said, quietly, then more brightly to turn down the guilt trip, 'Listen, it's fine here. I'm getting on really well with my gran. We watch DVDs together and she's funny and lovely and I'm really glad I've got to spend this time with her. I just miss you.'

'I would KILL to be there,' said Georgy. 'You know that.'

'I like our gang. Our gang of two,' Rain said. She heard raised voices in the garden and crossed the landing to look out of the window on the other side of the house. Vivienne and Harry were staggering under the weight of a huge tree and both laughing. She realised she wasn't going to spend another day sitting around not being involved in this. She carried on watching them as she finished talking to Georgina and then found a baggy pair of combat shorts and her comfiest Converses and went out.

'Right, I want to help!' Rain said. 'Today I'm going to help you both in the garden.'

Harry and Vivienne exchanged a glance.

'Okay,' Vivienne said. 'But no telling your father I'm working you like a common servant.'

'Hey!' Harry said, raising one eyebrow. Vivienne laughed.

'I've bought your soul, Harry, I'll call you whatever I like,' she said. 'Do you want to take a break and go and get us some lunch, and Rain and I'll fill the skip?'

Rain felt a small lurch of disappointment in her stomach because Harry was going.

'This place already looks so different,' she said to Vivienne.

'I know,' Vivienne said. 'I'm rather proud of us. Harry's a good kid, I got lucky finding him.' She tossed a roll of plastic bags at Rain, who caught it, to her own amazement – she'd spent her life being picked last for netball. Rain tore a bag off and copied Vivienne, who was filling her bag with small leafy branch cuttings. 'But I think we're going to need help for the inside.'

'Are you going to hire a proper decorator?' Rain said, again disappointed because this seemed to spell the end of Harry's help. The twigs spiked her hands but she didn't want to complain and look wimpy already.

'Oh no, I'm just going to see if he can haul in a friend of his to help. I know what I'm doing! It's just that I do want to get it over in the next few weeks and it's too much for two people.'

'Three!' Rain protested.

'Well, too much for three!' Vivienne said. 'Especially as I want to take you into town while you're here. Rather than stick you with the hardest work you've ever done.'

'Oh, this is not the hardest work I've ever done, thank you very much!' Rain said, mock-offended. 'I've just left a good Saturday job with Graydon-Hervey Shoes in the centre of Meersley. Average customer age seventy-five, and, if they've forgotten to wear their support stockings, I have to gently roll the snaggly, grey ancient pop sock over their blue corny feet. So it might be the hardest work *you've* ever done . . .'

'I can beat that.' Vivienne smiled. 'My first year as a student nurse and one of the patients, Mr Dalender, died with his mouth wide open. Matron told me and my friend Lucy to put his false teeth back in and get him ready for the morgue. But no matter how many times we pushed the teeth in, his jaw kept falling slack and the teeth dropped out again. By now Lucy and I were laughing hysterically and there was no way the patients outside couldn't hear us.'

Rain had started laughing so hard that she had to sit down on the warm grass. Vivienne sat down next to her and went on: 'So I had this brilliant idea of tying a bandage under his chin to the top of his head to keep his mouth shut. Lucy is tying the bow on the top, pulls too tightly, and the teeth shoot out. By now the pair of us have lost it completely. The other patients in the ward have seen us pull the curtains round him and now they're listening to us making these high-pitched squeaking noises – I couldn't even breathe any more – and then they see the teeth fly out through the tiny gap in the curtains.' Vivienne's voice was getting higher as she told the story. 'I peek out and grab them back, then we just shove them back in his mouth. This time they stay, and the mouth stays shut, but we still have to get him on to the trolley. The two of us – I was your age and about your weight, a skinny little thing – put his arms over our necks and try to heave together. But a dead body is *really* heavy and Mr Dalender was pretty fat, so he just keeled forward, and as he does that, he lets out this horrible loud GROAN! We nearly shat ourselves.'

'Oh my God he wasn't DEAD?' Rain said, thinking, 'Did my granny just say "shat"?'

'He *was* dead! But dead bodies still have air in their lungs and we'd squeezed it out – that's what made the groan. Of course we thought he'd come back to life and the pair of us screamed and I dropped him, his body lurched to the side then slowly out of the bed, and we scream again, then just stand there watching uselessly as his teeth roll out one more time.'

By now, Rain was cackling helplessly, crying and getting a stitch in her stomach, while Vivienne was making strange squealing guinea-pig noises along with her. At that moment, Harry came through the back door with their lunch and stood looking at them.

'Okay, I don't *want* to know,' Harry said. 'The pair of you just terrify me.'

Chapter 6

Sarah's diary

17 August

Why do I only write my diary when I am blissfully happy or suicidally depressed? The future me is going to think I only had two emotions! Mad ones at that! But I am, Older Sarah, perfectly, amazingly, madly happy today! It's midnight and I've just got in from the gig. I went with Nicola and I got to talk to QV again!

Rain felt her lips tighten and her eyebrows inch together. It was late, she'd been reading since midnight, but tonight she was losing herself in her mum's life. Sarah's first kiss aged fourteen on holiday in St Tropez, with a tall Irish boy who told her her lips were made for kissing, and she hadn't been able to stop giggling. Her fifteenth birthday, when Nicola had poured extra

71

alcohol into the punch Vivienne had made for them all, and Sarah had taken the blame. She was starting to get to know all the characters. Nicola wasn't a good friend to Sarah. In fact, in her opinion, Nicola was a flighty . . . well, bitch, who treated Sarah like crap far too often, expecting her to be there when she needed her, then ignoring her when other friends Nicola could use more came on the scene. Rain pulled the blankets tighter around her in bed, feeling suddenly cold. She read on.

QV is so perfect for me. I spend whole days after seeing him being excited and shivering with pleasure at the thought of things he's said – sort of whispering them out loud so I can hear them in my mouth – and remembering the way he looked at me when he said them. I come down with a case of grins, smile in that stupid uncontrollable way, sometimes I even start laughing JUST THINKING about being able to see him soon. We talk about things the same way – like we make jokes but don't laugh out loud at them, we just keep on talking, all deadpan. I love his voice and his face, and he gets me and he knows what's cool and what's not. He's read everything. He has this vast knowledge of Sixties bands – well, he's obviously going to be into music! – but he loves classical music, too. I think he likes me. I don't know if he likes me that way, but he's spent more time with me than he had to – he could have gone straight home tonight after his gig but he asked if I wanted him to see me home and I said no

because I didn't want to look pathetic – but was that a move?
What if he really wanted to walk me home and was put off
because I said no? And now he thinks I don't want to spend
any more time with him! OF COURSE I want to spend more
time with him but I didn't want him to go out of his way, I
didn't want him to be annoyed with me or think I was some
wimpy little sexist girly. So I said no, HOW STUPID am I?
Or maybe I did the right thing because it's better to play hard
to get because he's older than me and obviously out of my
league. Or maybe that was my ONE CHANCE and I BLEW
IT. Oh, please fancy me, QV, because I am going crazy over
you.

It was quite a sad turn in Sarah's story, really, because
Rain had looked at the date on the front of the diary,
and this was late in the year before Rain was born. In
just a couple of months – or less! – Sarah would meet
Sam Lindsay and fall in love with him, really in love,
and . . . the forecast for the following June would be
Rain. Rain sounded out the letter Q in her head. Qua,
quer, quee. Quentin was the only boy's name she could
think of.

Er . . . Quincy?

Or maybe it was a nickname, like a rap name:
Quali-T or something like that? 'After his gig', the
diary said, so he was some kind of musician? But was
Sarah writing too long ago for that sort of thing, rap

names like that? The trouble with Sarah's diaries was all the gaps – she'd write every day for a week, even two weeks, and the entries would stop for a month or even more and the cast would have changed and someone important would have come out of nowhere. This was the first time QV had been mentioned in the diary, and he'd come after one of the bigger gaps. As Sarah said, she tended to turn to it when she was very unhappy, putting down sad little entries about how Nicola hadn't asked her to some big social event, or how she wasn't pretty or funny, so no one would ever like her.

They were difficult for Rain to read. She had days like that, too; *everyone* did unless they were superconfident, and who was? But it was harder to think of her mum being sad when Rain was only just coming to terms with the thought of her mum being a real person. Before, when she'd thought of her, Rain's emotions had been rushes of warmth and safety; but also a huge, painful love she could never hold tightly enough, and that made her afraid. Something else, too – a dream-like, Princess Diana, fairy-tale sense of confusion, as if maybe it hadn't all been real. Now this: *too* real, too sad, too much emotion to put together.

4 September
So . . . . the fact is, he kissed me.

74

In the National Gallery!

We were in the room with the Caravaggios – the best room – sitting on one of the curvy leather seats looking at QV's favourite, and the place was totally empty. Except for the guard, who was a woman about my mum's age, and she was just slumped in her chair looking bored and deliberately not looking at us at all. We sat there for ages just talking and talking and laughing about the picture as if we were alone in our own living room – we were being a bit rowdy, actually, and I was convinced the guard would throw us out even though she wasn't looking, so I said shhh really quietly, and he repeated it back at me, taking the piss out of the quiet way I'd done it, and I gave him my meanest look, trying not to giggle, and he leaned forwards and kissed me. Just a little, soft, soft kiss, not some big snog like the boys my age would have tried to get away with. I pulled a shocked face at him, and he put both his hands up as if to say sorry. He didn't kiss me again. I overreacted! But I was joking, I didn't mean him to think I was genuinely offended. How do I make him kiss me again?

5 September
It's 3.15 a.m. and I'm still awake on the most perfect night of my life, and I don't want to go to bed because the moment I fall asleep it ends. We walked along the South Bank and held hands, stopping to kiss and look out across the river. It still looked like summer, but when twilight fell there was a bluey coolness in the air and I felt that time was rushing away from

us and started to get goose-bumpy. Q took off his coat and wrapped it around me, and the breeze from the river rippled his shirtsleeves but he wouldn't let me give him the coat back. Then we held each other and I've never felt like this about anyone before – it was like electricity passed between us. He was hugging me so tightly and I wasn't sure I was standing on the ground any more, and when I opened my eyes he was still right there with me and I couldn't believe I could be so lucky. How has this happened to me? This is love. It is LOVE. This is the love that people die for and kill for. But it can't be happening to me! I don't have feelings like that and, much more importantly, it is impossible that anyone could feel like that about me.

But when he holds me, when he kisses me, it's like our souls are touching.

I'm so tired but I can't sleep. I can't let this day end. This is our last weekend before school starts again and there will be no more days that are just ours, not for so long. I can't let this day end.

This isn't right, Rain thought. The year is wrong. Something's wrong.

6 September
Mum went unexpectedly crazy at me for coming in so late last night. I'd told her before I went that I was going to see the band play so she knew I was safe – well, you know what I

mean. Mum is pretty cool, and we have obviously talked about sex a lot – about the importance of condoms and how you should be sure that you're sure, and that you feel safe before going ahead and all of that. She acts like everything's okay if that's what I choose. But I think she really doesn't want me to do it, because she goes nuts when it looks like I might be. Hot and cold. Is everyone's mum like this?

Q called when I was crying and feeling dodgy, and it was like the previous day had been ruined. He said, 'What's wrong, what's wrong?' and thought it was him I was angry at, and I had to tell him it was my mum, and then he said something horrible about her and I was furious at him because I bloody LOVE my mum and I know why she goes nuts, and I hate it when anyone doesn't understand her. They don't even know each other, but they get so angry at each other. So now I'm angry at everyone and can't stop crying. The thing is maybe I don't know if I DO know enough about him to have sex, if we can still argue like this. But I argue with my mum all the time and we love each other. And I love Q. Even if I am angry with him right now. And angry at her. Angriest at myself.

Still 6 September
Q called again and said, 'Can we be friends?' I just stayed silent, listening to him breathing into the phone, holding my breath so he couldn't hear me breathing. He said, 'I'm sorry, Sarah.' I said what are you supposed to be sorry

about? He said, 'I didn't mean to be hard on your mum,
because I understand why she worries about you – she
loves you. And you can tell her why she shouldn't worry. I
love you too.'

He loves me.

I knew he loved me but to hear him say it! All my bones
seemed to go soft. It was like being kicked, but instead of pain
feeling warmth and peace and mad happiness.

But she's not going to have sex with him, Rain thought.
Rain's bones had gone soft, too. How can this be dad?
Dad wouldn't be in a band, he can't even sing! He's a
geek! This isn't dad. This isn't my dad.

7 September
First day back at school and it was surreal being a schoolgirl
again when I've just spent months out there in the real world
with a real life. Now things are like they used to be, but with
all the colour drained out of them. I have to smile at jokes
that don't seem funny any more, while the funniest person
I've ever met isn't there, and if he was he'd say something just
right after everyone else had finished laughing, then just me
and him would laugh. It's not good that I can't get on with my
friends the same way I did, and I really want to feel like I
used to feel, but at the same time I put on the laughter and try
to keep my head on the job. All I want to do is talk about
him, but I know I'd drive people mad. Besides, what we have

is for just us, I don't need to brag about it and stuff.

There are teachers again, people whose job it is to think you're wasting their time, and you have to call them 'miss' and 'sir' and ask permission to leave the room and I just want to say to them, 'It's over. You don't mean anything to me any more. Life isn't about iambic pentameters and quadratic equations, it's about the people you love.' If I said this to my friends they'd tell me to take my head out of my arse! Ha ha! And they'd be RIGHT. And I still don't care because I am in love. And I am loved.

I took some non-schooly clothes in with me and changed in the loos before I left, redid my make-up with all my pencils and lippies rattling in the sink, so I (hope I) looked okay when I met Q. It's still light quite late – the clocks haven't gone back yet – and still warm. We met at the statue of Eros (ahem) and went to a photography gallery near Leicester Square for the opening night party of a new exhibition there – a set of pictures taken in the Vietnam War, and they were beautiful but so sad and horrible that near the end I started crying and when I tried to blot the tears I smeared all my make-up and looked terrible. Afterwards, I didn't want to go anywhere fancy, so we got some chips and sat in Soho Square. It felt madly glamorous, though, going from an art opening to a shared tray of chips outside. A little old man tramp came up to us and said we made a lovely couple and asked when we were getting married. I felt my head boil up with blush and Q just smiled and neither of us said anything.

Maybe I should have said something so he didn't think I was thinking about it! Made a joke. Said, 'Not bloody likely!' or something.

But the truth is I could see myself with him for ever.

30 September
Last night I had sex with Q.

'No!'
Rain realised she'd said this out loud. She hoped no one had heard her.

'But you didn't!' she whispered. 'You're lying. And even if you're not lying you're going to meet my dad in no time at all and you're going to know what love is really like. You'll fall in love and it will be the *real* real thing. And I'm *proof* of that. You just have to hold on a little longer until he gets here.'

Last night I had sex with Q. Is there any other way of saying it? Slept with? That sounds like what old people do, people in their thirties and forties. Made love with? That sounds like what creepy old people do. Or people on Dynasty – Blake Carrington would have made love. We had sex. It hurt. Q kept saying, 'Are you okay?' and I told him how much it hurt and he stopped and I said I was okay, then he'd start again and it hurt more and didn't stop hurting until he'd finished, but I stopped telling him it hurt. But just before he'd finished, in amongst the pain, I felt something that might just also feel nice – really nice – but I couldn't focus on that feeling because of the pain. Then I got all weirdly giggly, and Q was upset because I was lying there laughing my head off, and then I was angry because he was upset and then I just started crying and couldn't stop. I acted like a complete freak. And then he held me, and said he loved me, and I closed my eyes and tears kept coming out of them, and I was making weird breathy sobbing noises that I couldn't stop making and I tried to stop all of it, the crying and the noises, but I couldn't. He lay there with me, kissing my cheek gently, stroking my hair back from my face, me with my eyes closed and my face wet with tears. Eventually I fell asleep.

I woke up not that long afterwards, it was still dark but I couldn't see my watch and didn't want to wake Q, so I don't know what time it was. He was lying with his arm over me, snoring, and I lifted my head to look at his face. I thought, yesterday I loved you, do I still love you today? I didn't hurt anywhere, but my mouth was woolly from the wine we'd drunk. Dawn was breaking and the room was cold. The bed seemed dirty, the mattress all thin and unevenly squashed, the sheets dark blue, and it was so far from the way I wanted things – a big high bed with white, white sheets and feather pillows, the morning all golden with bluebirds singing outside, and me smiling. I lay there and thought that I would never have this moment again. Then Q made a strange snotty sound and woke himself with a cough, and I looked around for places to hide, and he opened his eyes and looked at me, and for a moment his face was just . . . so innocent and so worried and lost and . . . beautiful. He found my eyes and looked into them, questioning, eyebrows shrugging, and then he winked and said, 'Morning, gorgeous.' And I knew how to answer my own question. Yes, I still love him today.

It was the last entry. Rain stared at it with eyes so dry that she could hear herself blink. Then she gasped, and started counting on her fingers.

PART TWO

Rain's diary

29 July

I can't ask Dad. I can't ask Gran. If I was born a month premature then there's a chance . . . but how could my mum have found my dad so soon after what I just read?

How could she have loved him?

I can only think that something must have happened between her and Q, like maybe he did something that made her hate him. Was he just trying to get her into bed and then, as soon as he had, he changed? Why did she stop writing?

And then I keep coming back to the obvious. It makes me sick with fear. I called Georgy, but she was all busy and shouting at her mum about whether she needed wellies because they're going on holiday tomorrow and I was too nervous and too ashamed to tell her. I don't even know what I mean by that – why would I be ashamed? My dad is my dad: he's the person I love most in the world and nothing is going to change that.

But does he know?

I didn't sleep last night. I tossed and turned and kicked and sighed, then I got out of bed and looked for a follow-up diary, one that mentions my dad, and then I surfed the net. Georgy won't have the internet or even any mobile reception where she's going, it's the middle of nowhere, because her mum wants her dad to forget about work and this is the only way she can get him to do it. And I've sent *my* dad on a working holiday because it's the only way I can get him to relax! I wish I could talk to Dad about it, but if he doesn't know – how could he NOT know? If my dad isn't my dad, she must have been pregnant when she met him . . . but she might not have known she was pregnant. Maybe even Sarah didn't know who my dad is! Oh, that's just STUPID and IMPOSSIBLE. Why didn't Mum keep writing? Can't ask Dad, can't ask Gran, I'm completely alone with this. Well, there's Harry, Harry's the only new person I know, but I'm not about to start telling him, he'd think I was some kind of basket-case. Well, maybe a stranger is the best person to tell . . . but not a stranger you sort of might fancy, probably. I've just got to keep this to myself, or even better, try not to think about it.

But how can I think about anything else?

Chapter 7

Harry was on his hands and knees when Rain found him in the living room the next morning: he was reading the instructions for an industrial-strength steam wallpaper-stripper which were opened out over the floor in front of him. Rain didn't speak for a moment: this was not because she didn't want Harry to know she was there. She was just so exhausted from the previous night's diary reading – and the shock and sleepless overthinking it had led to – that she felt quite a wreck this morning, and almost couldn't remember *how* to talk. Harry looked up and saw her and his face creased in a big smile, and she felt warmer all over and less like a wreck.

'Hey, here she is,' Harry said, so loudly that his voice boomed in the empty room. He stood up. 'Rain, this is Maddie. Maddie, Rain. I'm expecting you to get on because you both have weird names.' Rain looked where Harry was looking, at a very beautiful girl who was sitting behind Rain on the floor, long legs in jeans stretched out in front of her.

'Oi, you!' Maddie said, deftly throwing her balled-up hoodie at Harry so it hit him straight in the face and tumbled to his shoulder, where it hung without falling further. 'Rain is a *beautiful* name. And you should think before being rude to your boss, *Harry*. Hi, Rain, it's lovely to meet you.'

'Well, you too,' Rain said, feeling confused. 'Um . . . Maddie isn't weird at all, either.'

'It's short for Madrigal,' Harry said, removing Maddie's hoodie from his shoulder as if it was an unruly cat. 'It's pretty weird. We've roped Maddie in to speed us along with the interiors – remember Vivienne wanted us to get a move on and asked me to find help? I know she looks like a skinny posh girl who's never done a day's work in her life, but it turns out her Swiss finishing school did courses in Ancient Greek, etiquette, and spreading Polyfilla.'

'And judo,' Madrigal said, glaring at Harry with a pouty smirk. 'So watch it.'

Vivienne came in with a bucket full of decorating tools, from which she took some small paint-strippers.

'Any luck with the machine, Harry?' Vivienne said. 'I couldn't make head nor tail of it. Well, to be honest, I couldn't be bothered to read the manual, and it wasn't immediately obvious how it worked.'

'Yes, it should be pretty straightforward,' he said. 'As far as I can see, the only way it can go wrong is if your walls are made of chocolate.'

Vivienne laughed. 'Right, I'm going to go and make some tea. I'll keep the KitKats away from your steamer.'

'What have you got planned for today, Rain?' Harry said, when Vivienne had gone.

'Well, I'm helping here, obviously,' Rain said. 'Many hands make light work.'

'Ah, but too many cooks spoil the broth,' said Madrigal with a giggle. She pulled herself to her feet, and she was even taller than Rain expected. 'I expect you're dying to get out and see some proper shops, Rain! Harry said he took you to *Covent Garden*, and then to buy a chainsaw? Poor you, you're really getting a taste of the glamour of London, eh?'

Rain felt her stomach turn to dust. She'd had a great time with Harry and thought he liked being with her. But in fact he'd come straight back and told this . . . *girl* about it and couldn't have made it sound like much fun.

And, it was almost like this Madrigal was telling her to go away. Who the hell was she to tell Rain to leave her own grandmother's house? Surely when her gran had asked Harry to bring in another pair of hands, she'd meant another BOY! Otherwise, why couldn't Rain do whatever Madrigal was going to help them with? Rain was boiling with the kind of rage you only get when you're being weedy – when the only person you dare to give a hard time is yourself. She meekly left the room, though not the house, retreating upstairs. But in her bedroom she was trapped with the horrible secret she'd found in the diary. That her mum had loved someone who wasn't her dad at the time Rain was conceived. She needed to tell someone, she needed to shout it at someone, she needed someone to hold her by the shoulders and tell her everything was okay. And as Rain paced about the bedroom and stared desperately out of her window looking for that someone, she knew why she was so angry with Madrigal: she'd already wished it could be Harry.

There was a knock at the door and Vivienne walked in with a cup of tea.

'I told you I want to help, Gran,' Rain said. 'I thought I was doing okay in the garden. And before you say it, no I don't need to be going around seeing more of London, I need to be seeing more of my granny. Who I haven't seen for most of my life. So why is that girl here?' As she talked she heard her voice getting higher and closer to tears but she didn't care.

'That's why,' Vivienne said, looking at her granddaughter squarely, 'Madrigal is here. You and I are going shopping today.'

Rain grinned. 'Oh, okay.'

In the streets around Vivienne's house, Rain started

noticing a lot of the girls and women were dressed in a quite similar way and it was a much fancier way than she'd seen before – at home, and when she'd been out with Harry. There were a lot of beautiful dresses in bright colours with expensive shoes and bags, and Rain started to feel hot and dowdy in her jeans.

'Maybe I should have worn a dress,' she said at one point to Vivienne, really just thinking aloud.

'Do you want to pop back and change?' Vivienne said. 'It is going to be hot today and we're not far from home.'

'I don't think I've got a dress with me!' Rain said. 'Well, I know I haven't because I don't actually own any dresses.'

'We should do something about that,' Vivienne said. 'Everyone needs dresses. Oh, don't look at me like that, Rain!'

'I don't really know that I'm a dress person,' Rain said, blushing. 'You know how some people are jeans people and . . . '

'No, I don't think so, not you,' Vivienne said, turning down a small road to the right. 'You'll see – there's a shop along here and you're going to want everything.'

Rain wouldn't willingly have gone into a 'boutique' shop in Meersley, because they tended to look like charity shops that only sold beige clothes and might have smelled of cats. De Facto was nothing like that. It was like a cool girl's boudoir, with little crystal chandeliers and chaise longues, long ornate mirrors and curtains and gorgeous velvet-tied necklaces thrown casually on counters. An icily-beautiful Japanese assistant was lounging near the window, flicking through a magazine. When Vivienne held up a dress and asked about it, she came over in a second, nodding excitedly about how much the dress would suit Rain and stagily whispering that they'd sold one like this to Keira Knightley. Rain had never tried on anything this expensive: she knew she wasn't going to buy anything, but it was really nice dressing up and having someone with her who made her brave enough to be there. Vivienne leaned against the wall and when Rain came out of the changing rooms in various outfits she said things like, 'Oh, you could be Mary Tyler Moore' and, 'No, no, the trouble with that one, if I'm being honest, is you look like a call girl. A *nice* call girl, though.' Rain looked really different in dresses like this: not like herself – tidier and older, in a way that she loved. She'd always been on the scruffy side, but here she was in a little sugar-pink Sixties-style number looking like – well, not quite like Vivienne said, but not like a teenager who dressed down in old comfy jeans and dressed up in new dressy jeans.

'Let me buy this one for you,' Vivienne said, when Rain emerged in a gorgeous grey shift dress with little cap sleeves. It had a prim little white Peter Pan collar, and a killer-short A-line skirt.

'Oh, Gran, I love it, but the truth is I'm never going to go anywhere posh enough to wear it.'

'You'll be going to places with me that are posh enough to wear it! Besides, that's nonsense, it's just a little everywhere everything dress. You could wear it to Tesco.'

Rain argued and Vivienne paid, and Rain only felt a little bit guilty walking out with her boxy cardboard bag, because Vivienne was so sweet and dismissive about buying it. Rain thought that this must be what shopping with your mum was like. She felt a sudden sad-angry pang because she'd never really had the chance to do it with her own mum, whereas her friends luxuriously tried to get out of shopping with their mums or got indulgently stroppy with them. After years of hardly seeing her gran, she now had this moment with her, and she wasn't going to waste it on feeling sad.

They stopped at a little eat-in deli and had really good toasted club sandwiches with fat, hot chips (Rain insisted on paying) and Rain was enjoying herself so much that she could almost for a moment forget that she'd just run head first into the biggest identity crisis of her life, and she was going to have to talk about it or she'd explode.

She leaned away from the table and studied her granny's face: still pretty, with soft skin and lines only in smiley places. No. She couldn't ask her about it.

When they got back to the house, the living room walls were almost completely stripped. Madrigal was alone in the living room, her blond hair falling over her face as she picked wallpaper-mulch off her scraper. She looked up, saw Rain's carrier bag and said, 'Oooh, De Facto, how posh! Let me see!' and although she was just being friendly, Rain was intimidated and, weirdly, *upset* by the easy, immediate closeness, and she didn't want to show this older London girl what she'd got in case it was wrong, somehow.

She hesitated then took the dress out, and as she unfolded the rustly tissue paper it was safely gorgeous.

Madrigal whistled admiringly and said, '*Stunning.* Harry and I are going to have to find somewhere to take you in that.'

Harry and I. That probably meant they were a couple. Rain felt a throb of pain and caught her breath when she realised she was jealous. Could it really be jealousy? Had she fallen for Harry, with his dark beauty and unexpected kindness, and fondness for taking the piss out of her?

'You've done masses,' Rain said, looking at the walls. 'I should get changed and come down and help.

I bet you could both do with a break.' She wanted to ask where Harry was, but now she was frightened even to mention him, as if the way she said his name would give something away about her feelings for him.

'Oh, we're still going strong,' Madrigal said. 'We should have done this whole room by the end of today . . . well, although it may mean staying till bedtime.'

Rain had a feeling that Madrigal was trying to tell her not to come and help. Obviously, if she needed the money and Rain came and shortened the job, Maddie *wouldn't* want her there. But Rain wanted to help her granny, and Vivienne usually spent most of her time working on the house and she wanted to be with her, not to go out on her own. She stood there hesitantly, trying to make a decision.

Rain took her dress upstairs and put it on a hanger, which she carefully hung on the outside of the wardrobe door so she could look at it. She loved it. She saw the diary she'd been reading the night before on her bedside table and picked it up again, wondering if she'd been so tired when she read it that she saw something that wasn't there. Before long she was as engrossed as she had been the first time she read it: she sat on the floor, her lips moving as she whispered her mother's thoughts aloud, her eyes filling with tears.

There was a knock at her door and Rain hid the diary under her bed and called, 'Come in, Gran,' while wiping her face dry with her sleeve and hoping she looked normal.

'It's not your gran,' Harry said from the other side of the door.

'Oh!' Rain said, getting up and opening the door herself. She gave him a friendly smile when she saw him, but he looked at her and frowned.

'Everything okay?' Harry said.

'Yeah. What's up?' Rain said, as brightly as she could.

'Your gran thought as we're working so late tonight that we could all go out together for supper. So we're taking a vote on where to go. Madrigal thinks Indian, your granny says sausage and mash, and I'm . . . Are you sure you're okay?'

She nodded, unable to speak because she always got pointlessly emotional when people felt sorry for her, and her voice would have given her away. But Harry moved forward anyway and somehow pulled her into a gentle hug, and Rain's head seemed to fall on to his chest and fit perfectly, while his arms held her just enough and she let herself go soft in them.

'Hey, what's wrong?' he whispered into her hair.

'I'm just . . . missing my dad,' she said. 'He emailed me, just made me a bit weepy, that's all.'

'This is the first time you've been away from home, isn't it?' Harry said, and his hug loosened and Rain stepped out of it, feeling the loss of his warmth. 'It's very normal, and I'm sorry I walked in while you were . . . having a moment. Don't be embarrassed. Now listen, your gran's sausage and mash idea isn't bad, but now that I've got you alone, I think I can get you on to my side. I happen to know this amazing Persian restaurant just . . . Rain, what's wrong?'

'I told you,' Rain said. She gave him a very direct look, repeating slowly: 'I just miss my . . . '

'Have you had bad news? Has something happened?'

'Not recently,' Rain said, with an attempt at a laugh that sounded horrendously un-laugh-like. Harry stepped into her room, and she told him everything.

When Rain and Harry came downstairs again, they didn't realise that they both looked quite guilty because they were keeping a secret. Madrigal gave Harry a questioning look and said, 'Well, you took long enough! What's the decision?'

'What decision?' Harry said.

'What are we *eating*?' Madrigal said.

Rain and Harry glanced at each other. As soon as Rain had started talking about the diary, they hadn't mentioned food again.

'Rain was convinced by my Persian suggestion,' Harry said.

'No, no,' Madrigal said. 'You had her alone up there

too long. I think you tortured her into agreeing with you. I'm joining Vivienne's sausage and mash team, so that's two against two.'

'Three against one,' Rain said, trying to sound normal. 'I want to be on the girls' team.'

'Ha!' Vivienne said. 'Good girl. Tough luck, Harry.'

They walked in two pairs, Vivienne and Rain together and Harry and Madrigal behind. Rain wondered if Harry would tell Madrigal what they'd been talking about in her room. Maybe Madrigal would make fun of her and Harry would laugh, because Madrigal was his girlfriend. Obviously it wouldn't be ideal if Madrigal knew, but Rain had really needed to talk and Georgina was in the remote Highlands, and, once she'd started, it had turned out that Harry had been a very easy person to talk to. He was enough of a stranger for her to be interested in his reaction – how weird the story would sound to someone else. But she knew enough about the way he talked now to have some idea of how truthful that reaction was. He hadn't been freaked out at all. 'Oh listen, one day I'll tell you about some of the scandals in my family,' he'd said, as they sat next to each other on the floor beside her bed, looking at their feet. 'My great granddad was a bigamist, for one.'

'Well, but,' Rain had said, ignoring his smile, 'it's my mum. And my dad.'

'I know,' Harry had said, his face serious again. 'It's not the same.'

As she walked with her granny she only kept one ear on the conversation, and tried to imagine what Harry had meant by that. It must have been one of those things people say, particularly boys, because boys always tried to come up with solutions whereas girls were better at sympathy. She could hear Madrigal laughing and couldn't shake her paranoia. Gah, she didn't want Madrigal to know! Why had she trusted Harry?

Over dinner Madrigal squeezed Harry's hand sometimes, when she was talking to him, and at one point even reached over and teasingly pulled his cheeks together with her finger and thumb. Rain realised she hadn't said a word for ages, and that her face was set in a frown; she hurriedly relaxed it. This really *wasn't* jealousy, she decided, it was just that perhaps she shouldn't have trusted Harry when she hardly knew him and hadn't even liked him a few days before.

But he had listened so nicely. There was surely no mistaking that dark, true gaze. She had no idea why she'd suddenly opened up to him, but she was glad she had. Rain pulled herself together and got back into the conversation, hiding her inner conflict behind pretend confidence and jokes.

Chapter 8

Rain got a text at nine the next morning. She was writing an email to her dad that she'd re-started about fifty times, an email that was definitely not going to mention the diary. Her head was still fuzzy from the glass of red wine she'd drunk the night before with dinner, and she'd showered but let her hair dry any way it liked. The text said, 'I'm outside. Wondered if you want to chat again. It's okay if you're busy or would rather not. Harry.' She thought about how nice he'd been the night before, when she'd talked about her dad. Since then, she'd been worrying about having made a fool of herself. She was afraid she'd talked too much about things that were probably a bit embarrassing for a near-stranger to listen to, although he'd listened nicely. She blushed when she thought about it, and screwed up her eyes.

Rain and Harry had swapped mobile numbers early

in the day when they went to get the chainsaw together, in case they'd split up and then lost each other, but the text came as a surprise.

'It's Saturday,' Rain texted back. 'Don't you have anything better to do?'

'Nothing comes close,' Harry texted. 'Now can I come in, it's raining out here.'

Rain glanced out of the window. It was raining quite hard. She could also see the outline of her hair reflected in the glass: it wasn't good, but hey, so what? She went downstairs to see Harry.

Her grandmother had left a note on the kitchen table that said: 'Gone to supermarket for big stuff. Text me if there's something I'm likely to forget. Text me anyway to remind me to get garlic, I ALWAYS forget.' Rain let Harry in the kitchen door and sat down at the table to write the garlic text to Vivienne.

'How are you feeling?' Harry said, pulling out a chair and sitting across from her.

'Fine. I've drunk wine before,' Rain said, pressing send on the phone and looking up at him.

Harry smiled somewhere over his shoulder. 'I meant, how are you feeling about what you told me yesterday,' he said. 'I'm sure you're a really *champion* drinker, though.'

Rain hid her own smile because she didn't want him to know she found him funny. She had already decided not to mention the diaries to Harry again, or anything personal like that. He had a gorgeous and slightly possessive girlfriend. She didn't want to risk starting to really fancy him and making a fool of herself, trusting him like a boyfriend and then having to back off when the real love interest was around. She didn't want the cool student couple gossiping about her while they were washing magnolia emulsion out of their hair together, being intimate and loved-up.

'I shouldn't have told you,' Rain said. 'It was . . . silly. I'd just had a shock and I can't call my best friend, she's unreachable this summer. I'm honestly absolutely fine. People's lives are complicated. My family's no exception. I mean, there's Vivienne, she's had two husbands, I don't know if . . . '

'Look, you don't have to explain anything,' Harry said. 'I hope you're okay.'

'Of course!' Rain said, throwing her arms up a little wildly. He tilted his head sideways to gauge her okayness. 'I mean, I sort of didn't sleep and stuff, but, you know it's . . . '

'Yeah, it's, um . . . ' Harry said. 'It's a pretty big deal.'

'The thing is,' Rain said, finding herself unable to stop again, 'I just don't know what to do about it. I feel like I won't be able to stop thinking about it until I know the truth, but I don't know who does know, and if I ask the wrong person I could really mess up.'

'There's not really very much you can do without asking people, though, is there?'

Rain slumped forward, her head in her hands. 'That's it. It's depressing, but it's just something I'll have to do or not.'

'Okay, well. You know. Good luck,' Harry said. 'And if I can do *anything*, I'm always happy to listen and stuff.'

'Thanks.' There was an awkward pause.

'I was, I was sort of thinking, though,' Harry said. 'Did you think about any specific name when you were reading through the diary?'

'No,' Rain said. 'My parents moved from London not long after that and I don't think they're in touch with anyone they knew from back then. Why?'

'Oh, it's nothing, it's stupid,' Harry said. It looked to Rain as if he was *not* saying something else.

'What?' she said. 'Is there something I should be doing? I really don't know where to start. I don't know who any of the names are, so there's no one I could ask.'

'Really, it's not my business,' Harry said. Again, he looked evasive.

'But what?'

'I didn't say "but".'

'You sort of seemed about to. Look, *tell* me what

you think, *please.* Even if it's nuts, I promise it can only help.'

'Well . . . ' Harry sighed. 'No, it's . . . ' Rain gasped in frustration, and then Harry suddenly blurted: 'Have you heard of Quentin Vienna?'

'Er . . . *yeah.* But I don't know why? Who is he? What's he got to do with my mum? Oh, right, his initials are QV. You think it's him, then? Who is he?' Rain was talking in a joky, bossy way, but she could see that Harry looked rather serious.

'He's a singer. *Was* a singer. I, sort of, went home last night and you know sometimes if you hear initials you put words to them, like you fill in the words, even if you don't know what the initials are for?'

Rain didn't do that. She bit her bottom lip and looked at him, waiting for him to finish.

'So I just . . . didn't stop thinking about it. Even when we were all out together, I wasn't really keeping my mind on the conversation, I just kept coming up with the same name for the initials and, hey, shall I make some coffee? Do you fancy some coffee?'

'And it was . . . *Quentin Vienna?*'

'Yeah. I mean, he's not *famous,* but I know his music. He sang in a band you probably won't know. They had about two hits, neatly avoiding being labelled one-hit-wonders – all well before your time.'

'But not before yours?' Rain said, playfully. 'What

104

was the band? You're saying my dad was a pop star? What would he be doing going out with a schoolgirl?'

'Oh, listen, I don't know,' Harry said, pulling away from the conversation again. 'It's pretty stupid, I guess. It's just that you trusted me with something important and I was worried it was because you didn't have anyone else you could tell – and I took it seriously because you were. I just thought if I told you it might spark off some memory.'

'No. I'm really glad you told me,' Rain said. 'It . . . doesn't. But I mean, nothing does. I'm sure he's not . . . my dad, and everything, but thanks for thinking about it. I mean, there must be a million QV people out . . . '

'Yeah, that's the funny thing,' Harry said. 'The – really, let's get some coffee – point is, the initials *are* too weird. No one else has those initials. Well, okay, there are actually lots of people, I went through the phone book . . . ' He stood up and went to fill the kettle with water.

'You went through the phone book?' Rain looked at the back of his head as he stood at the sink.

'Er . . . yeah. Does that seem weird?' He didn't turn round to look at her as he asked.

'Um . . . no?'

Rain heard Harry chuckle. 'Well, God damn it, I did, anyway. It turns out there are literally hundreds of people with surnames beginning with V – Vaughans,

Vales, Vincents. Some of those, but not many, have Q initials. It's really not many. And it's all in alphabetical order, so it didn't take me very long. You could check it yourself . . . '

'And you came back to this singer, Quentin Vienna?'

'Well, it's the year before you were born, so, I think we're talking about a year before his band was big, not that they were ever really big. It's possible.'

Rain was about to ask more questions, then stopped suddenly and her stomach lurched as she realised she was almost beginning to enjoy herself. What they were talking about was dead serious – it was *real*. Her mum would have been torn to pieces when it happened, when the man she had fallen in love with somehow had to leave her. It turned Rain's own identity on its head, it would make her question things she thought she knew about herself and her life.

It would break her dad's heart.

Rain sank back in her chair and remembered the pain and tried not to feel the excitement. But her heart was galloping inside her still slumped body.

'What if I don't want to know?' she said, her voice husky.

Harry brought the coffee cups to the table, and Rain breathed in the warm smell. 'I shouldn't have said anything,' he said. 'You know who you have to talk to. And it's definitely not me.'

106

The silence stretched and Rain heard the clock in the hall ticking.

'If you go now,' Rain said, blowing on her coffee, 'you know and I know that I'll just go straight to my computer and look up Quentin Vienna on Wikipedia, and I'll wish you were here to ask things because you seem to know what you're talking about better than me. You've told me now and I can't put the genie back in the bottle.'

Harry gently held her forearm in his hand without taking his eyes off her face. The warmth of his touch on her skin made her shiver. 'I don't know anything,' he said. 'It was just silly speculation. You can forget it because you *know* I don't know anything.'

'But what if you do,' Rain said. 'What if this is right?'

'Well,' Harry said. 'Before we worry about that, I think you should get your laptop.'

Quentin Vienna (singer)
From Wikipedia, the free encyclopedia

Background information

Origin	England
Genre(s)	Synth Pop
Label(s)	Fruitgum Records
Associated acts	Lavender Sandcastles
Website	Unknown

Quentin Vienna is a songwriter and singer known for his work in Lavender Sandcastles, a retro indie band with heavy Synth influences, active during the Nineties.

Lavender Sandcastles

Before they started their project Lavender Sandcastles, Quentin Vienna (vocals) and Marv Higson (keyboard) were playing in a band called Primitive Grip. Later on they left that band and they started writing with new band member Danny Redstone (guitar). They were contacted by Fruitgum Records and got a contract with the label. They were joined by Kelvin Culhane (bass) and Jeff Riesling (drums and percussion). Their first hit single was 'Elemental' from their debut album Lavender Sandcastles, which reached number 3 in the British charts and was number 1 in Sweden, Finland and Norway. The following year they released Belinda's Destiny which would be their last album. The first single from that album, 'Can't Face You', reached number 10 in the British charts.

Later Years

After the band broke up, Quentin Vienna left the music business.

'That is . . . *interesting*, my mum has both those albums and she used to play their songs when I was a kid,' Rain said. Her heart and pounding head seemed simultaneously flooded with panic and adrenaline. 'But that's got to be true of millions of women her age, hasn't it?'

Harry gave a little shrug. 'Yeah. Thousands, maybe.'

Rain tried to find some more revealing links, but

there was just page after page of identical hits telling her how to buy their songs, brief discographies on geek music sites, the videos on YouTube and Google, and some pictures that *would* have been funny, with terrible clothes and hair-cuts, but were now weird and jarring. She stared at the close-ups of Quentin Vienna's face.

'He doesn't look like me, though. Does he?' Rain said. She *could* see a resemblance, but she didn't want to.

'He . . . well, he does,' Harry said. 'You can see it, I can see it. Look at this one.' He clicked back to a window at the back of fifty other pictures of Quentin Vienna. He had blond hair and Rain was a brunette, and Rain's dad had brown hair and her mum had had dark blond hair . . . but Quentin's was clearly dyed. His eyes were similar to Rain's – hazel-brown, not much lid showing, low brows. Her chin had a little dimple in it like the one Quentin Vienna was thoughtfully rubbing in some of his pictures. Rain took a knife out the kitchen drawer and studied her reflection, as if she needed a reminder. Meanwhile, Harry waited quietly, and she realised how silly she looked, staring at herself and trying to find a stranger.

'Look at his ears,' Harry said.

Rain touched her own ears with her fingers. 'Well, who looks at ears?' she said. Harry shrugged. But Rain could see exactly what he meant.

'You don't really have any big reason to think I'm Quentin Vienna's daughter? My mum had the albums and the initials are QV, that's it?' Rain had to work hard to say this in an offhand way, as if she was making fun of him and herself, and wasn't feeling let down. But her eyes gave her away.

'Well, look, don't think I'm completely barking,' Harry said, picking up a bag he'd slung under the table earlier, 'but there was sort of one other thing I did.' He took out his phone. 'I . . . well, I downloaded a couple of their songs.'

'Quentin Vienna's songs?' Rain said, looking at him with wide eyes.

'Lavender Sandcastles. Yeah. I mean, just because I knew them and wanted to hear them again and I'd started thinking about them. And this one's interesting.' Harry found the track on his phone – it was called 'Not My Baby' and they both listened to it through the tinny little speaker.

'I can't hear what he's . . . ' Rain began, but Harry made little shushing gestures with his fingers.

When it was finished, Harry said, 'Neither can I, not all of it, but I think we should try to work it out. I looked on lyrics sites, but it's not there, probably because it wasn't a single.'

'Hang on, let me get a pen and something to write on.' She brought two pens and Harry started the

110

song again. Three or four listens later, they'd got it.

You don't get my life it's not your life
Maybe you're braver than me
Or maybe you just don't know what it's like out there
I'm scared for you but I can't do this with you
So someone else will be holding my baby
Someone else will be teaching my baby to smile

Have to tell the world this is not my baby
Though I love you more than any other boy ever will
Have to let the world think this is not my baby
If you knew how much I love you you'd never let me go

You want more than I can give you
You say it's easy and I laugh then you laugh
But I saw you last week with that guy
The one with the hair and the stupid look
And someone else will be holding my baby
Someone else will be teaching my baby to smile

Have to tell the world this is not my baby
Though I love you more than any other boy ever will
Have to let the world think this is not my baby
If you knew how much I love you you'd never let me go

'You know baby never means baby in pop songs,' Rain said.

'Mostly not,' Harry agreed.

Rain read through the lyrics again, frowning and pulling little strips of skin off her lips.

'I just don't think it's enough,' she said, looking up at Harry with a tiny blob of blood in the middle of her mouth.

'You're, er, bleeding,' Harry said.

'Oh sorry,' Rain said, rubbing her lips with her fingers, which came away bloody. 'I do that. I do some weird stuff sometimes.'

'Everyone does,' Harry said, nodding.

They heard the door open and Vivienne was back from the supermarket, carrying heavy bags. Rain had all the clearest pictures of Quentin Vienna open on her computer, and their transcriptions of the song were spread in front of them. The little phone rattled as 'Not My Baby' played for the fiftieth time.

'What are you two up to? Homework?' Vivienne said.

Rain closed the laptop a bit too hastily, just as Harry grabbed for his phone and turned off the song.

'Well, take your faces out of the internet, it's Saturday,' Vivienne said, heaving a huge bag of potatoes on to the kitchen table.

'Let me help you with those bags, Vivienne,' Harry said. 'Can I make you a cup of tea?'

'So, Harry, why are *you* here today?' Vivienne said.

She started pulling things out of her cotton carrier bags, until the table was crowded with fruit and delicious-looking pastries and bread. Rain hadn't eaten any breakfast yet and grabbed a croissant, while listening to the rest of the conversation. She was feeling a bit lost for words because they'd been doing something she didn't want Vivienne to know about.

'I fancied going to the Tate Modern today to see the new Andy Warhol exhibition and wondered if Rain wanted to come along,' Harry said. 'Although I know it's the weekend and you may both have something else planned.'

'Actually, I would *love* it if you both got out of here for the rest of the day.' Vivienne was stacking yoghurts in the fridge and she whirled around, smiling. 'I really need a haircut so I thought I'd drag Rain along with me to the Red Door, but quite honestly, it's not cool enough for her.'

'What's the Red Door?' Rain said.

'It's a salon thing in Mayfair,' Vivienne said. 'I used to go a bonkers-number of years ago, and probably everyone I knew then will have gone and it'll all be different and depressing, but . . . ' She looked thoughtful. 'Anyway, if I can palm you off it'd be even better, I can take my time without feeling guilty. I'd like a manicure, too – my hands are manly after all that gardening.'

'Terrific,' Harry said. 'And your hands are still very

dainty. Are you taking a 23? We can all get the bus together.'

'Oh, good idea,' Vivienne said. 'You two can cross the river at St. Paul's.'

'Exactly,' said Harry.

'I'll just get changed, so I don't scare their chi-chi customers,' Vivienne said. She vanished into the hall.

Harry and Rain looked at each other as they waited for her.

'You're very quiet,' Harry said. The arrival of Vivienne seemed to have loosened him up: he seemed back to normal, teasey Harry again. 'Although I suppose you think it's rude to talk while you're absolutely stuffing your face with croissant.'

Rain immediately gulped the mouthful down. 'Maybe I just got a bit freaked out seeing how quickly you came up with that lie.'

'It wasn't a lie!' Harry said, laughing. 'Look!' He pulled a crinkled *Time Out* from his pocket, which was open on an article about the exhibition he'd mentioned.

'Oh, that's convenient,' Rain said. 'But you were obviously planning on taking Madrigal and just improvised.'

'I thought it'd be a good idea to spend a day away from this house to talk things over, if you wanted to. And it's a good place to do that, you'll see. Why would I lie?' Harry said.

Rain bit her croissant again. 'I don't know,' she mumbled as she chewed.

'Well, look, I should probably just go,' Harry said. 'In fact, that's probably best because you've got a lot to think about, more than you wanted to, and I think I've only complicated it . . . '

'But . . . I don't think I want to go on without you,' Rain said. 'I'd like to talk about it some more. If that's okay?'

Harry paused. 'So you're going to love the Tate,' he said, grinning.

Rain's diary

30 July

I keep staring at the Lavender Sandcastles albums and thinking, are you totally nuts, Rain? I keep looking into Quentin's eyes, trying to see if he has a message for me. Are they like my eyes at all?

My weird days, my weird summer, my weird life. I'm feeling closer than ever to knowing my mum this summer . . . but at the same time she's throwing unbelievable shocks at me. I'm having something that feels quite like a romance . . . but I know the boy can't be mine. I think the hardest part of all of this is having to go through it all without my dad. Today I miss him more than ever before, so hard it hurts . . . but I have to start accepting that he isn't my dad, and maybe at the end of this, when we're together again and everything should be fantastic, I'll have to tell him.

Harry and I went to the Tate Modern today. We took the bus to St Paul's, which is all plump and pretty like a cake, and walked across the Millennium Bridge, which is shiny silver and seems really fragile compared to all those big scary Thames bridges that cars go over. It's very windy, so my rubbish hair flew about and this either made it look worse or better. And there's a bloke at the other end trying to sell you whistles that make bird sounds who you have to sort of ignore by pretending your mind is on higher, artistic things. Quite honestly I was terrified of going into an art gallery with Harry because I don't know the first thing about art. I was worried we'd stand there in silence and he'd say something about abstract or cubism, or ask me what century Anthonyo da Vinci was painting in and I wouldn't know *anything*, so he'd secretly think I was an idiot and want to run away.

We went inside and it was the most amazing thing I've seen since I got here. A massive hall, giant, bigger than any room, really high, really long, the floor all painted like a chessboard with black and white squares, and tons of little kids running around with silly bowler hats and moptop wigs, screaming with laughter and having a fab time with their parents and each other. I was just standing there with a slack jaw thinking – *this is an art gallery*? They also had more of my new worst fear . . . living statues. Harry said, 'Oh no. Can you try to control yourself with the statue people this time?'

Then we just messed about. We watched the kids, we wandered around. I even understood the art! I think. I mean, there's not that much to understand. The name gives you a clue and it's more about feeling whatever you feel when you look at it. The Warhol pictures were stunning – just these simple photographs, but some of them made me weirdly emotional, like a series of prints of electric chairs. Then as we walked back through the other rooms there was a grand piano hanging from the ceiling which suddenly seemed like it was about to fall on our heads when we walked under it – all the keys fell out and I jumped a mile, and we had to leave the room because we were laughing too much. I wondered if my friends back home would take the piss if they knew what I was doing, because this summer, no one is going to be wandering round art galleries, that's for sure. They'll just be having a laugh, drinking cider by the river, going to Blackpool for the day. And I *love* that stuff.

Sooner or later, though, I guess you have to do something else.

My mum went to art galleries with him – the summer she got pregnant with me.

We went ages without talking about QV and I got nervous, wondering whether Harry was avoiding the subject now or what. It wasn't till we went to the café and we'd got our drinks and some bread with mezze and dips to share, that Harry quietly drummed his hands on the table and said, 'Okay, Miss Rain, what's our plan?'

'What are we supposed to do?' I said, 'The Wiki entry didn't give us anything. I don't suppose Quentin Vienna was in the phone book?'

Harry said, 'No. It's probably not his real name, it doesn't sound very real. But I bet Madrigal could help.' I don't know what my face looked like, but it must have given away something, because Harry said, 'Oh, hey, I'm not going to tell her anything. Her dad's this really rich estate agent now, but he used to be big in the music industry at exactly the right time for Quentin Vienna, so I'm guessing he still has some contacts.'

'If her dad's so rich,' I said, 'why is Madrigal spending her summer doing decorating work?'

Harry looked like he was about to answer, but he just changed the subject and started talking about the London music scene twenty years ago. I couldn't think of anything except Madrigal finding out about my life.

'How are you going to not tell her? She'll want to know why you're asking – what ARE you asking?' and Harry smiled in this sort of pretend secretive way and I suddenly got angry. I said, 'Look, this is serious and it's horrible. When I'm with you it's easy to forget what we're actually doing and it just seems like, nearly like fun, and then as soon as you're gone I remember and it's *not* fun, it's nothing like fun. And then I want to stop and run away and go back home to my dad, except he's not there and I don't know who he'll be when he gets back. I don't think I can keep doing this Miss Marple investigates thing.'

Harry said, 'Rain, the only way you're going to stay sane if you do this is to remember every minute of every day that your dad is your dad. And he loves you. And you love him. What we're doing now is . . . just like when people trace their family trees – but it is NOT YOU. You haven't changed. You're still you.'

I got all whiny and said, 'Family trees are about people you never knew. This isn't like that. *Everything* has changed! You just don't understand,' feeling totally stupid as I was saying it, but I couldn't stop myself.

'Well, tell me how you're going to NOT find out.' he said. 'Tell me how you're going to go back home and carry on with your life and not spend every moment wondering what the truth is.'

I shoved dry bread in my mouth, which was

suddenly sore because I wanted to cry. I could hardly swallow. I said, 'Please stop pushing. I don't care. I wish I'd never read the diary and I don't want to know any more.'

'I'm sorry,' Harry said. 'I didn't mean to push you, that's the last thing you need. I was trying to keep things light, but look, it was a mistake. I KNOW this is really big, life changing. I just thought I could help. I think you're great.'

And I, like some total dick, started crying.

From: s.lindsay@zoctine.com
Subject: I miss you too
Date: 31 July 08.10 a.m.
To: rain@zoctine.com

Rainy, I don't know what I did to deserve such a sweet email – probably being so far away from me for so long has made you forget what an infuriating absent-minded neglectful dad I am. But I miss you very much too. It's Sunday, which means you and I would normally be making our way through a mountain of papers and a hill of fried bread. The thought of that is making me homesick. You're the only reason I want the summer to go quickly. It's strange reading emails from you when we've never been apart before and we've always just communicated in half-sentences and shorthand while going about our normal days together. I've meant to tell you since we started sending emails to each other that you write very well and you're super-smart, a lot better than me at this kind of thing. I think maybe you'll never be a scientist, but I'm not worried about you at all. Other parents worry all the time about their kids, and I never have, but not because I don't love you. I'm very proud of you, Rainy.

Love Dad

Chapter 9

On Monday morning, Rain was up early, nervously waiting for Harry to come and start work. She astonished her granny by bringing her breakfast in bed. Well, a pot of tea and a piece of hot buttered toast. Vivienne looked very pretty first thing in the morning, her wavy silver hair falling over her face, her blue eyes brighter without make-up around them. Rain opened Vivienne's heavy, faded curtains, letting in the dappled sunlight that filtered through the tall trees that Vivienne and Harry had left alone, and sat on the edge of her gran's bed, casually looking through the jewellery and perfume bottles on the bedside table.

'How're things?' Vivienne said.

'Things're good,' Rain said brightly, taking the stopper out of a tiny round bottle made of indigo glass. The perfume inside smelled of violets and dark chocolate. 'I've never even heard of this one,' Rain said.

'It's not easy to come by,' Vivienne said. 'Your grandfather used to buy it for me. It's from an odd little French perfumery, and they still make it but they don't sell it in Britain.'

'My granddad or Philip?' Rain said, referring to Vivienne's second husband.

'Rain,' Vivienne said. 'I don't mix them up!'

'Yeah, sorry, of course,' Rain mumbled. She felt embarrassed: before this summer she would never have said anything like that, but she thought about things differently now. She put her nose to the perfume bottle again. 'Did you love them both as much? Do you mind me asking that?'

'No, I don't mind,' Vivienne said. 'And . . . no.'

'*No?*'

'No. I wish I had, but I still think of your grandfather as the love of my life. Ed was just . . . *me*, you know? But with added blokey things that made him fun to be around. Now I'm back in London after such a big gap, it's hard seeing the places we went to, without him. When I see them again, the first thing I think about is the last time I was with him there.'

'Do you think there is only one true love for everyone, then?'

Vivienne leaned forwards so her elbows were

123

resting on her knees. 'No, of course not. I fell in love again when I was married to Philip, for one thing.'

'With someone else? Bloody hell, what happened? Did he love you too?'

Vivienne smiled wonkily. 'Yes.' She shrugged. 'Nothing happened. We were both married. I did love Philip, you know, it just wasn't *the thing*. He was a lot older than me, and he was what I needed at the time, someone very grounded and easy-going, someone to stay indoors with. I would never have hurt him, or been cheap enough to be unfaithful, so . . . we just . . . had a good laugh about what terrible luck we had, me and the other man, and I cried in the bath for a week or two, and then I let him go.'

'I've never been in love,' Rain said. She didn't know what to say after her granny's revelation; she didn't think she could talk about it with her as if they were both adults. 'I don't think I have, anyway. I've never felt like people do in films and songs. Sometimes I wonder if I even could fall in love, I think I may have something emotional missing. When I've gone out with boys I haven't really felt *anything*, except that it's a bit of a pain having to decide where to go and what to do, and having to pretend to your friends that it's going to last FOR EVER when I know it isn't.'

Vivienne snorted. 'Pff. I'm afraid I think you're just like the rest of us, Rain, and you'll fall in love horribly easily as soon as you meet someone good enough for you.'

'I wish.'

'Count on it.'

The doorbell rang and Rain jumped so much that she knocked over the now-empty cup on Vivienne's tray. 'That's Harry,' she said.

Vivienne was in the middle of an indulgent yawn. 'D'you fancy letting him in so I can lounge around a bit longer?'

'Yeah, of course,' Rain said. She didn't know why she was so nervously excited, but there was no mistaking the thumpiness of her heart or the silly smile that kept tugging at her lips. Was she expecting Harry to walk in with her real father or something? He was just as likely to have bad news, or no news.

She smeared a little lip balm on before she opened the door . . . to Madrigal.

'Oh, hi Madrigal,' she said, and tried to glance past her.

'Harry's going to be late,' Madrigal said.

'Oh. Fine,' Rain said. 'Come in. Can I . . . make you some tea?'

'Oh yeah, that would be great – could you use my herbal teabag, though?' Madrigal said, giving her a little grey-green sachet.

'Sure,' Rain said. When she came back up with a mug of boiling water that the herbal teabag had barely coloured at all, Madrigal was just wearing a bra with her jeans. Rain gaped – not least because Madrigal had the most perfect and rather huge breasts she'd ever seen – and then realised that she was just pulling off her jumper and had accidentally pulled off her T-shirt underneath with it. Her stomach was concave under her ribs, and her knickers, just visible above the jeans, were bright candy-pink with blue lacy edging. Rain tried not to stare as Madrigal tugged the T-shirt back down.

'I'm happy to make a start on my own,' Madrigal said. 'Have you got the radio?'

'Oh. Yeah, sure,' Rain said, and fetched the radio they usually listened to when they were doing housework. Madrigal took it from her and turned it to an indie music station, then carefully set it down on the floor by her jumper.

'Thanks,' she said, and started pulling the teabag in and out of the pale water, not looking at Rain.

That was it. They weren't friends. When the others weren't there, they weren't going to talk.

Rain felt too embarrassed to stay. She muttered something about having to go upstairs for something, when Madrigal suddenly said, 'Oh, Harry asked me your pop star question. Funny! Well, he'll tell you, but

I think I put him on the right track. I was surprised he knew anything about the Sandcastles, but I suppose I shouldn't have been. Harry has always had the worst taste in music. I've learned to . . . well, *tolerate* it would be the best word. But you have to put up with each other's lapses of taste, don't you?' She paused, as if this wasn't a rhetorical question.

'Yes, I suppose you do,' Rain said.

'Harry is just as annoyed by my constant checking of celebrity gossip websites,' Madrigal said.

'Haha, yeah,' Rain said. She needed to get away. Unlike Madrigal, she wasn't being paid to be here.

'How was the Warhol, by the way?' Madrigal said.

'Oh,' Rain said, surprised by the question. 'Really nice. I thought some of the . . . er, paintings were really . . . er, great.' She was sick of sounding like an idiot, but her brain seemed to be freezing every time she had to answer Madrigal. It was like staring at a blank screen waiting for a web page to load, and then getting an error message.

'And what would you say were the highlights?' Madrigal said, suddenly staring straight at her. It felt like being quizzed by her maths teacher!

Rain returned the stare. 'The Coke bottles,' she said, breathing heavily through her nostrils, as if she was being surly in class.

There was a pause and then Madrigal said, bouncily:

'Well, great, I'm glad he found someone to go with him after I let him down; that was the last day that exhibition was on, you know. And Harry's never liked going to art galleries alone, he likes discussing the show and thinking it through out loud.' She turned her back on Rain completely and started getting on with the wall stripping.

Now, finally, Rain's brain was filling with cool retorts that she just couldn't say out loud because they'd have been rude. She wanted to tell Madrigal that she knew what was going on: that she was a little rich girl who didn't have to be here, playing at having a job for the summer just to hang out with her boyfriend, and that Rain got the message, she couldn't have him, fine! She didn't *want* him! But behind those protests would be the truth: Rain *did* like Harry. She did want to spend more time with him. She felt fizzy when he made fun of her. She'd loved it when he'd almost bounced with excitement when they'd been caught up with looking at pictures of Quentin Vienna together, Harry pointing to the album covers and saying, 'He looks like you, too, I'm not making it up! Those are your ears!'

That nice memory was muddied now by the fact he'd gone off and talked to Madrigal about everything. Rain understood exactly why he'd had to; that it would be natural to explain to your girlfriend what you'd been doing – and Harry had *told* Rain that was what he was going to do, he'd said Madrigal's dad and his music industry contacts might be able to put him on the right track. But after hearing Madrigal's smooth, clear warnings, Rain felt young and dumb. The embarrassment steamed inside her until it turned into anger. How could Harry have been so careless when he must have known how much this mattered to her and that she'd want it kept a secret?

She jumped when Harry knocked on the window and waved from outside at both of them. Madrigal went to let him in, and when she was in the hall, Rain grabbed her chance and got out of their way, slipping behind and up the stairs.

A little later, Harry came up to see her. Rain opened the door with a pair of sandals in her hand and told him she was just on her way out.

'Oh,' Harry said, sounding disappointed. 'But I've got some news so . . . when are you going to be back, do you think?'

'What sort of news?' Rain said. Her plan had been to stay frosty with him, so that he had some idea that he'd done the wrong thing, and would back off. But even though she felt mad at him and betrayed, and still felt the edge of Madrigal's obvious warnings, she wished above all that she could pull him into her room and start whispering with him about whatever he knew.

'I've found Quentin,' he said.

Rain sat on the floor, because she knew if she carried on looking straight at him she'd smile, and started putting her sandals on. 'Well, that's very clever, but aren't you forgetting we have literally no reason to think he's QV?'

'Well, not *no* reason,' Harry said. 'I mean, you know he's in a band. His initials. 'Not My Baby'. The fact your mum has the albums. Your, er, ears . . . '

Rain touched her ears. 'All ears look the same! And even if they don't, what kind of resemblance is ears? I look like my mum.'

'You look like him too.'

'It's not enough.'

'But why not start with him?'

'We can't go and ask everyone with those initials, that would be insane.'

'Well, what else does it say in the diaries?'

'There's nothing else in them, nothing else about who he is or how she knows him.' She shrugged. Harry sat down with her, his thigh touching hers, and she looked at his lean, dark profile and had a sudden, mad urge to grab his shoulder and throw herself into his arms. 'You can look at them if you want?'

'I don't think that's a good idea,' Harry said. 'They're private. Look, I should get back and do what your gran pays me to do.'

Rain held her toes in her fingers. 'Where's Madrigal?'

'Downstairs, stripping,' Harry said, and Rain thought of the gorgeous body she'd seen first thing this morning and knew that she didn't have a chance with him.

'Why don't you just read the last one?' Rain said. 'I mean, if it doesn't creep you out. It may be I'm just missing something.'

Harry shrugged. 'Look, I just think it's a bit . . .'

'I know, I'm being obsessive. Let's pretend I'm not nuts.' She took the notebook off her bed and flicked through the pages. Then she handed it to him. Harry shut the book, but he took it.

'So where did you find Quentin Vienna?' Rain said. 'Is his address in the phone book?'

'I don't have his address yet,' Harry said, 'but I have his name. His real name.'

'Which is?'

'Colin.'

131

Chapter 10

'Huxnjjd ehsuihf hsdrh efhuhu.'

'I can't hear you!'

'HUXNJJD EHSUIHF HSDRH EFHUHU.'

'I can't hear you, where are you?'

'Can you hear me now?'

'Yes I can hear you now.'

'I'm outside the National Gallery. You have to get here now. Huxnjjd ehsuihf hsdrh efhuhu.'

The line went dead. Rain waited, staring at her mobile. Harry rang back.

'Sorry about that. You have to come to the National Gallery now. I've FOUND THE PROOF.'

'What proof? How do I get there?'

'Take a 23 bus.'

'What sort of proof? Do my ears look like the Mona Lisa's?' Rain laughed at her own joke.

'The Mona Lisa's in the Louvre, you fool. You're

132

going to see it, and you're going to be amazed and you're going to apologise!'

'But it's seven o'clock, when does it close?'

'It's Wednesday, it's open late tonight. Till at least eight, maybe nine, when can you get here? Oh, I suppose you'll be eating supper soon.'

'I don't think Gran'd mind, we were only going to have the rest of the deli salads she left you for lunch today, she isn't cooking.'

'Then get on the bus! I'll go and wait in the Pret over the road, call me when you get close.'

Rain had given Harry her mum's diary and she wasn't sure why; she couldn't think of a good reason now. In fact, she could think of a few bad reasons: she'd started worrying he thought it was weird of her, because he hadn't got back to her, until now. She hadn't seen him on his own for a couple of days. Vivienne had been taking her out in the daytime to her favourite places in London – today it had been Soho, where her gran had once had a flat (!) and where they made their way past little market stalls and XXX-rated bars with neon naked-woman-shaped signs outside, and then ate delicious, tiny dim sum in a super-trendy restaurant. In their absence, Madrigal and Harry had been dutifully stripping the huge, high ground-floor walls on their own. Rain knew how hard the work was, and felt bad

133

about it when she and her gran came in late and the two students looked totally flat-out exhausted, sitting at the bottom of the ladder with massive piles of torn grey wallpaper pieces around them. Still, it was a summer job, and they had both wanted to do it. Probably, in fact, they'd spent half the day snogging, so Rain had nothing to feel bad about. Actually, she admitted to herself, it was precisely that, the probable-snogging, that she felt bad about.

But Harry hadn't said anything about the diary, and, although Rain wasn't surprised, she'd been disappointed when he came to work and didn't take a detour past her room and excitedly explain his latest theory. Had he got something to tell her now?

Rain found her granny eating olives and reading a magazine at the kitchen table, and told her that Harry had asked if she wanted to go and meet him.

'I think he suddenly got last minute tickets to something or something like that,' Rain said, realising this was a lie that was only going to get more complicated later, but she couldn't come up with anything else. She took an olive so she'd have thinking time while she chewed.

'How are you getting on with Harry?' Vivienne said. 'He must fancy you tons, I think.'

Rain almost inhaled the olive. She started coughing. 'Oh, Gran, he doesn't, what about Madrigal?'

'What about Madrigal?'

'They're totally girlfriend and boyfriend!'

'Oh, she *wishes*,' her granny said.

'Really? You think they're not a couple? Do you know that?'

'Well they haven't *talked* about it, but it seems obvious to me.'

'But it seems obvious to me that they *are*,' Rain said. 'They kept holding hands when we went out for dinner.'

'*She* kept holding *his* hand.'

'I didn't notice him objecting.'

'He was probably being polite. I just can't see him with someone like Madrigal,' Vivienne said. 'She's really not very funny, she's just . . . *pretty*. That's so boring.'

'Yeah sure,' Rain thought, 'gorgeous blondes probably aren't his "type", he'd rather have a good old-fashioned belly-laugh.' There were some things grandmothers just weren't going to understand, even very hip ones like Vivienne.

'So is it okay if I go?' Rain asked.

'Yes, go! But look, I'm telling you, I still think Harry fancies you. So if you don't fancy him, be warned.'

'Right, Gran,' Rain said and, even though she knew it was completely impossible and stupid for her to even think about, she smiled all the way to the bus stop, and only stopped smiling because a weird-looking man with lots of laundry bags on the other side of the road noticed and smiled back at her.

Rain was just a touch more nervous about going on the bus alone in the evening, but as soon as she got aboard, she realised it was just the same as the daytime bus – packed with the same mix of people: two elderly Arab men reading the same foreign paper together, a crazy old lady filling out both sides of her seat with knotted carrier bags, people of all ages and all races ignoring each other. And it smelt faintly of sick. She asked the nice-looking Chinese girl next to her if she could tell her when the National Gallery stop was coming up and the girl said she was getting off before then. Rain didn't dare ask anyone else, and kept her eyes fixed to the road, nervous that she'd miss it, but a few minutes after the Chinese girl had got off, a little old man two seats away turned around and said to Rain, 'Excuse me, love, were you asking about the National Gallery? It's the next stop. This is Trafalgar Square.'

She thanked him and rang the bell. As she hopped over the massive gap between bus and pavement, she was already punching Harry's number into her phone. She waved at the old man from outside the bus.

'Okay, I'm at Trafalgar Square,' Rain said.

'Fantastic!' Harry said. 'Stay right where you are!'

She looked around her, trying to see across the still-crowded Trafalgar Square, feeling a little lost. They'd gone past it before on the bus, but now she was there she realised she should have made Harry tell her exactly where they were meeting. The roads around the square were jammed with fuming traffic. The buildings on all sides were very tall and white and she wasn't even sure which direction she'd come from, or where she should be going, or how Harry would find her, everything was too big. She stood still for a moment, watching kids climbing all over the big lions at the foot of Nelson's Column, and little toddlers getting out of their buggies to chase the pigeons, screaming with laughter. There were loads of pigeons and when they flew up away from the toddlers in frightened clouds, Rain ducked and let out a little scream, holding her hands over her face, feeling the sweep of dusty wings against them.

Then she saw Harry, breaking into a little skippy run every three or four steps, brushing his hair back and, when he saw her, smiling.

'This had better be worth it,' she warned him.

'This,' Harry said, 'could be dynamite.'

It was funny how they could both talk quite lightly now about Rain's terrible bombshell discovery, and Harry didn't worry about hurting her feelings, and Rain didn't worry, as she initially had, about the fact that her feelings should be hurt when Harry was flippant about it. But moments like this didn't really feel much to do with anything real, they just felt like the crazy thing she was doing this summer.

'This is going to prove that "Colin" is my dad, is it?'

'You're making fun of me,' Harry said, raising an eyebrow and smiling. 'But get ready to take me seriously.'

'It could be dynamite,' Rain said.

Harry held her hand and pulled her arm. 'This way.'

He opened the door for her, and, going straight past the reception desk, led her through lots of dark, woody rooms with warm red wallpaper. The gallery was still quite full, with groups of students sitting on the floor, some of them sketching paintings. The floors creaked as Harry and Rain walked behind them. Finally they came to a much bigger room with soothing green wallpaper, bright with natural light. Harry took a step back, and flamboyantly waved his arm towards a picture. It was one of the smallest pictures in the room. It showed a plump androgynous young man with a pink rose in his hair holding his hands up in weedy horror and pain as a little reptile hung from his finger.

'What am I looking at?' Rain said. 'A fat boy playing with a newt?'

'Maybe you could read the title?' Harry said, failing to hide how much Rain had amused him.

'*Boy Bitten By A Lizard . . .* ?' Rain read. 'BITTEN BY A LIZARD! That's a Lavender Sandcastles song! It's on *Belinda's Destiny*!'

'Aha,' Harry said.

'But that's . . . ' Rain took a step closer to the picture and stared at it. It was a very beautiful picture, with a crystal-clear vase of water and glossy succulent fruit in front of the boy. 'But actually . . . what's that got to do with anything? "Colin" named a song after a picture, so what?'

'Did you see who painted it?'

Rain leaned forward again. 'Caravaggio?' Her eyes widened. 'Caravaggio, it's in the diary, it's, er . . . ' She couldn't remember why her mum had mentioned it.

'And this one too?'

Rain leaned across to the next painting, which was much bigger, and looked familiar, she felt it must be quite a famous one. '*The Supper at Emmaus* . . . Caravaggio, Michelangelo Merisi da.' She read it slowly, trying to remember.

'Let's sit down.' Harry was carrying a newspaper, and he carefully opened it and took Sarah's diary out of its folds. There was a paper bookmark in its pages, and Harry turned to the marked page and gave Rain the book.

4 September

So . . . the fact is, he kissed me.

In the National Gallery!

We were in the room with the Caravaggios – the best room – sitting on one of the curvy leather seats looking at QV's favourite, and the place was totally empty.

'It's this room? It's this room!' Rain said.

'Boom,' Harry whispered.

'But even so,' Rain said. 'Where does it say *this* is his favourite picture? It just says favourite picture.'

'You're a tough crowd,' Harry said. 'His initials are a not very common QV. We know this bloke plays in a band. He takes her to fancy gallery openings. He has an encyclopedic knowledge of Sixties music – the influence of which some might say can be heard in the retro-Sixties melodies of the two-hit wonder band Lavender Sandcastles, who recorded the song "Not My Baby". And his favourite picture is *in this very room* which doesn't have many pictures, but one of them has the same weird name as a Lavender Sandcastles track. Seriously, what more do you want?'

Rain pushed her lower lip out in an unconscious pout. 'My mum to tell me it's him . . . ' she mumbled.

'How about if *he* tells you?'

'What?'

'I told you I found out Quentin Vienna's real name.

I think we can track him down and we can go and have a chat, and if he knew your mum then . . . '

'But how? Oh, Madrigal, I suppose.'

'Yeah, yeah, Madrigal'll help, of course she will!'

Rain remembered with a jolt that she'd been angry with Harry for sharing the story with Madrigal. She wasn't angry any more, not when Harry was doing so much for her. He was being lovely. But she still felt sick to the stomach that Madrigal was involved, and this could never be more than a larky summer mystery to Harry. If he could get his girlfriend to help him play detective, it would be even more fun for him.

'Well, I suppose we could . . . *talk* to him . . . about . . . ' Rain tried to find the words. 'No, this is just insane! We can't go hassling some stranger who's also sort of famous, he'll think we're complete nutters. He probably still has groupies camped outside his house.'

'I have to say, that's incredibly unlikely. Seventeen-year-old groupies even more incredibly unlikely. They weren't a massive band. Most people haven't heard of them.'

'But he's still not going to see us.'

'At this point,' Harry said, 'he's just some bloke who was in a band when he was a kid. There are thousands of old pop stars alive today, and they don't go around acting like Elton John. So we just don't know. He might.'

Rain breathed out loudly, half-laugh, half-exasperation. She was sitting in the seat where her real parents first kissed, with a boy she wanted to kiss her. Instead of kissing her, he was talking crazy talk to her that seemed to drift in and out of making sense.

Harry gave her a little smile. 'What's the harm in asking?'

Downstairs in the café, Rain had managed to come up with a more competent list of questions.

'He must have known, she must have told him, and he didn't stay with her. Why bring back what must have been an awful time in his life? What if he has a wife now, and he has to tell her and they can never be the same again? And if I find something out, how can I not tell my dad? I would never be able to keep something like that from him.' Rain looked into her cup because she knew she'd cry if she had to face Harry when she said the next thing. 'Last week, no one hurt at all. What gives me the right to hurt other people this week?'

Harry tilted his head on one side. His dark brown eyes were warm, but she felt herself shiver. 'You're not trying to hurt anyone,' he said. 'You're just trying to make sense of things.'

Rain's diary

6 August

I can't sleep. It's 4.22 a.m. and I haven't slept yet. I flopped around in bed until the restlessness made me want to kick my legs until they couldn't kick any more. Then I started looking out the window, which was a mistake; the street is empty and lonely and dark with strange shadows, it just makes me even more scared and I feel scared anyway. Harry only told me this evening that we were on for tomorrow. There were a few days where he didn't have any news at all: I was disappointed, but relieved too, because part of me didn't want to go any further, wanted it to be so hard I just gave up.

What if tomorrow changes me? It's bad enough today, not knowing anything – yet knowing there's more to know. Now that it's happening, I've started thinking about it seriously and the questions I keep coming back to feel like stones in my stomach. Does he know? If he knew, why did he let me go? If he knows, he doesn't want to see me – so what will happen when he's forced to?

And if he isn't the one, how long do I have to keep looking?

I keep thinking, I can't stop my head thinking. I know that in all this the one person I don't want to be hurt is my dad, my *proper* dad, Sam Lindsay. Does he know? If he doesn't, do I have to tell him? Or can I only find out he knows by asking him, by which point it will be too late? When I think of him being sad because he's found out, or because he knows I've found out, I almost can't hold everything I feel in my head at once, it's a junkyard of shame and regret, I'm aching all over at the thought of doing something that's going to cause him pain. He is the person I love most in the world, and whatever train of events threw us together, he's the biggest part of me, what makes me me. It's his sense of honour and sense of humour that I've absorbed, his amazing kindness that I've always seen as the sort to try for. Yes, he's a brilliant scientist and I got a C at GCSE chemistry, but you know what? I am also virtually tone deaf and can't play an instrument to save my life, so I don't have anything of the other bloke either, and I know that genes aren't what made me and my dad so close.

Even as I write this, I'm terrified that opening up the past will somehow let my dad stop loving me. I know it's stupid, but it's such a big fear, the worst and biggest, that the tiny odds don't matter – God, there aren't even any odds! I have to stop thinking that way! But I can't . . . I don't want the other man, not for a second, if it'll risk what I have with my dad. So why am I doing this, and why is Harry involved? *It's not his life.*

And Harry, who's responsible for tomorrow, who

has pestered Madrigal's posh dad and somehow talked a former pop star into spending his Saturday evening talking to a teenage girl, God, what do I do about Harry? It feels a lot like I'm falling in love with him. I once read an old saying in a romance book:

To love is nothing
To be loved is something
To love and be loved is everything.

What I have right now is the beginning of nothing. When I'm not thinking about my dad and bloody Quentin Vienna, I am playing back in my head all the things Harry has ever said to me, every smile, every look, every accidental or friendly touch. It's partly to obsessively analyse it and try to work out how he feels and what he meant by it, and partly because, when I replay the smiles, the looks, the touches, I start glowing all over again and can't feel my feet . . . and I want to laugh out loud.

Gah, it's *stupid*! He's got a girlfriend! But I can't help that he makes me happy. I sound like a tired person now. I'm writing like someone who is stupid with tired and doesn't even know what the words mean. I need to sleep or I'll talk like this tomorrow. If I just sleep through tomorrow, will Harry come and tell me how it went and who I'm supposed to be now?

Chapter 11

'I can't drag you and you can't keep hiding behind me,' Harry said. 'People will see. People will think I'm your abusive boyfriend. Come on, Rain, he's expecting us and we'll be late.'

Rain tried to stay on her feet without moving, while Harry pulled her. She hid behind him again, burying her face in his shoulder. He smelled clean and just noticeably citrussy. She didn't want to lift her head off him, she didn't want to see people who might be looking at her. She was being a nightmare and she knew it, but couldn't stop.

'Hey, Rain,' Harry said very gently. 'Do you want to go home? If you want to go home right now, it's totally okay.' He tried to look over his shoulder at her. Rain shook her head into Harry's shoulder. 'What do we do?' he said.

It was seven in the evening, but as sunny as it had

been at noon, the kind of evening Rain liked to spend entirely out of doors, because being inside was a waste of summer. They were in Camden, which was very different from Notting Hill. It was younger and untidier. There were more drunk people, tattoos and piercings, girls with shaved heads and boys with pink hair, but there was a sweetness to the atmosphere, almost a last day at school feeling, when everyone looked more like themselves but the bullies left them alone because they were in a good mood. And Rain's erratic behaviour wasn't really standing out as she and Harry fitfully made their way through the streets.

'Can't you do it for me, without me?' she said. 'We're too close now, he might walk down the street, he might look out of the window and see us.'

'I'll go without you if you want, but I think it's a bad idea,' Harry said. 'But if that's your decision, I'll do it. I'm right here with you and I won't go anywhere unless you want me to.'

'Of course I don't want you to go!' Rain said. 'Tell me again exactly what you told him, *exactly* how much he knows and what you're going to say . . . '

'What *you're* going to say . . . '

'NO. I'm not going to say anything. You're going to say everything and I'm going to hide behind you. Or it's ALL OFF. We may as well go back now because I can't, there's no way, I'm not going to say anything.

We'll just sit there in silence if it's up to me, it's not going to be up to me, I'm not doing it.'

'I told him . . . '

'It's *definitely* him? Madrigal's dad is sure? Because Colin Thurber isn't a very unusual-sounding name.'

'It's definitely him. You can make that your first question! Were you Quentin Vienna? If he says no, you don't even have to ask him the rest of the questions!'

'So what did you tell him?'

'I told him that we found him through Madrigal's dad, who used to manage two of the bands that the Sandcastles supported. He remembered Big Roy . . . '

'Big *Roy*?'

'Er, Mr Madrigal used to be known as Big Roy, apparently.' Rain smothered a smirk. Big Roy didn't sound very *Madrigal*-esque. ' . . . and we wondered if he could spare a few minutes to talk about the year he was doing the *Belinda* tour, as research for a university project.'

'What, you *lied*?'

'Yes.'

'What? Why? He's going to be horrified and he hasn't been warned!'

'Well, I did warn him as well. I said there was also something more serious we wanted to talk about that happened around that time, but it was probably best not to talk about it over the phone first.'

'What did he say?' Rain said.

'He asked if it was bad news, and I said no.'

'It IS bad news! For him it is terrible news!'

'It isn't bad news. For all you know he's spent the last seventeen years wishing you'd try to find him.'

They crossed the road and Rain tripped over the kerb. As the pavement zoomed towards her face, Harry grabbed her and pulled her up at the last minute, almost tearing her T-shirt at the neck.

'Are you okay?' Harry said, keeping hold of her shoulders. 'Rain, if there's really a chance this is going to kill you, I'll just take you back home. Vivienne will kill me if your heart stops in there.' Rain blinked at him with tired eyes. The heat of his touch shot all the way through her.

'Let's go,' she said.

'In there or home?'

'In there,' she said, her voice all croaky. 'But you have to do the talking.'

Colin Thurber's house was a tiny little Victorian terrace on a street that looked like it had once belonged to poor people and had now been poshed up. The front door didn't have a doorbell, just an old-fashioned knocker. Harry knocked twice, hard. Rain flinched both times. Harry touched her back with his palm; it was just a little touch, but it kept her from fainting. She changed her mind more than twenty times as they waited for someone to answer the door, the nervousness building inside her and making her want to shout something out loud, or just run as fast as she could, anywhere. In moments, Rain might be looking straight into the eyes of her real father. What would he look like now? What would he think of her? She shut her eyes and said a last-minute prayer that he wouldn't hate her.

A handsome middle-aged man opened the door. He didn't look anything like Quentin Vienna – he was black and very tall, and Quentin Vienna wasn't either of those things.

'Hi – Harry? And Rain? I'm Anthony,' the man said. He smiled. 'Col won't be long, he's in the middle of something in the kitchen – we're having some friends round later. Come in, he told me you'd be here now.'

Rain's stomach twisted. She pushed Harry in first, so hard he almost tripped over the step himself. Anthony led them into the living room. The house seemed much bigger on the inside than it had looked from outside. It was decorated in a pretty and modern way – the walls were bathed in light and painted a warm sunflower yellow. There were slightly knobbly stripped wood floors, and two fat gold corduroy sofas. The windows were open wide and there were fresh flowers. The television was enormous. The cooking smell was almost delicious, but was shot through with a slight suggestion of something possibly burning somewhere.

'Rain's such a pretty name,' Anthony said.

'Oh, thanks,' Rain said.

'Well, please, sit down. I'll just go and hurry Col along. Would you like tea?'

'Yes, please,' they both said.

When Anthony had gone, Rain grabbed Harry's hand. She would never have dared do it normally, but there'd been a lot of touching between them today, a lot of falling and shoving and hiding and clutching and she was finding it easy to be rough with him now. 'We can't stay,' she whispered. 'They're expecting people. They think we'll be gone in five minutes! I can't stop talking about it in five minutes. We have to *go.*'

'What are you talking about? We're here now!' Harry whispered.

'You told me I didn't have to go through with it. Well, I want out.'

'It's too late now. Look, he said to come at this time, so he must be okay for a bit.'

'Harry,' Rain said out loud, standing up. Harry stayed where he was, looking up at her, smiling. 'Are you really not coming with me?'

'I told you, I'll do the talking. Sit down. Be quiet.'

Rain pretended to be shocked by Harry's straight-talking, but she was grateful that he'd taken away the choice and sat down again. Anthony came back with tea.

'I think the cooking is going quite well,' Anthony said. 'So there won't be any plate smashing and screaming.' He caught Rain's expression and smiled. 'I'm just joking,' he said. 'You're both at Imperial, right? Col said you were here doing some kind of research into the pop scene when he was in it. He's had students writing to him in the past, once or twice, and he's never talked to them before, but he told me he owed Big Roy a favour. You've got to love Big Roy. What's the project you're working on?' Rain listened to the lies Harry had told stacking up and thought she might have to make some kind of sound – a scream, a yelp, something.

'Well, look, I really have to come clean about something straight away,' Harry said. 'We're not just here for the research, or at least, well, it's quite a bit more complicated than that.'

Anthony frowned, and said, 'Yeah? Go on . . . ?'

'I think he's my real father,' Rain blurted out, as if she was joking. But Harry actually gasped, which made Anthony gasp too, more loudly than Harry. Rain immediately felt ashamed of making everyone gasp.

'I thought I was going to do the talking,' Harry said. 'I'm not saying I'd have done it better. But . . . you have a way of going straight to the unsayable.'

'I'm going to get Col,' Anthony said. 'I think I should probably leave you and him alone for this.' He put the tray down without giving them their mugs of tea. A few seconds later, Colin Thurber – Quentin Vienna – came into the room without Anthony. He had a thin body under a round, double-chinned face. His dark hair was threaded with silver at the temples and sideburns. He was wearing tight stone-washed jeans and a flowery shirt with the buttons undone quite low. He was nice-looking for a man in his forties, although he was also wearing eyeliner.

'What's the story, kids?' Colin Thurber said, cheerfully but nervously. 'Ant said I had to get in here fast.'

'Seventeen years ago,' Rain said, 'my mother gave birth to me. All I know is that she spent the summer with an older man . . . ' She couldn't stop herself now, it was as though nothing normal and polite could come out, only these surreal, crazy-sounding things.

'We're terribly sorry to intrude on you like this,' Harry said. 'Do you remember a girl called Sarah Devonshire?'

Colin Thurber sat down on the sofa opposite Harry and Rain.

'No, I'm sorry,' he said, frowning with confusion, still trying to be friendly. 'But I'm terrible with names, do you have a picture? Maybe if you tell me what this is about, too, I can help you with what you're looking for.'

Anthony had come back into the room. 'Col, they think you're this girl's father . . . ' He must have been listening to the conversation the whole time. He shrugged at Colin Thurber and threw him an anxious look, but stayed at the door, not fully joining them again.

Colin Thurber's eyes widened. Rain felt hers widening along with them. She braced herself. Then his shoulders hunched forward jerkily and he sniffed and Rain realised he was laughing.

'You can see I live with a man?' he said. He turned towards Anthony and smiled at him. Anthony smiled back hesitantly, pressing his lips together sympathetically as he looked over to Rain.

'I hope this doesn't sound rude, but it wouldn't be unheard of for a gay man to have a child with a woman,' Harry said. Rain stared at Harry, trying to work out if he was even a little surprised, as his voice betrayed nothing.

'No, that's true,' Colin Thurber said. 'But I would definitely remember if I'd had sex with one.' He gave a little laugh, but looked shy, as if he wasn't all that used to telling complete strangers personal things about his sex life. 'Which, er, I haven't.'

Anthony came further into the room and sat down

next to Colin. Rain and Harry were both silent. There didn't seem to be anything to say. They could hardly argue with him.

'Why did you think I was your father?' Colin said. 'Is it . . . what your mum's told you? I'm sure she wouldn't lie to you, but Colin Thurber isn't a very uncommon name, so it may just be that you have the wrong Colin Thurber.'

'It wasn't my mum,' Rain said. 'I mean, it was but she didn't tell me, she's dead. It was in her diary.' She *knew*, she *knew* how ridiculous she sounded now. She needed to look at the diary again – it must have been one of those teenage girl wish-fulfilment fantasies and not a word of it was true. But it had seemed so real. And why would Sarah have been lying that way at the same time she was beginning the most important relationship of her life?

Anthony pressed a mug of tea into her hand, and because it had been sitting around for a while it was at the perfect temperature to drink quickly. Rain knocked it back, not stopping till she was at the bottom of the cup, delaying the moment she'd be expected to talk again. She was feeling really stupid. She looked around her, at all the photographs of Anthony and Colin together.

Harry had the diary in his inside coat pocket and he took it out.

'Can I take a look?' Colin said. Harry glanced at Rain, who nodded, and he passed it to Quentin Vienna.

'You know,' Rain said, painfully. 'It doesn't even say your name.'

'Why did you think it was supposed to be me? Just the initials?' Colin was turning the pages slowly, looking for entries that might have explained why he had two strangers bringing a paternity suit in his living room.

'There was a picture, or sort of a reference to a picture... *Boy Bitten By A Lizard*,' Rain said, her voice getting quieter.

'Well, it's a ... famous gay picture,' Colin said. 'It's symbolic. It was one of the songs I covertly come out in. Not that I was ever really in, I never told *Smash Hits* I had girlfriends or anything like that. And your real father likes that picture?'

Rain bit her lip.

'And in fact ... she doesn't say it's *that* Caravaggio,' Colin said, quietly, without looking up from the diary.

'We were listening to 'Not My Baby' as well and ... I guess it's not really about a baby,' Harry said. Rain suddenly remembered her mum singing 'Silver Begins'. The memory hurt now, and she didn't say anything.

Colin laughed, but not unkindly. 'No, it was about my first love,' he said, and his face softened until he looked quite like a teenager as he talked. 'He was an older boy at school and he tried to persuade me that it'd be okay if we went out . . . But I was too afraid. Too afraid of being discovered, and – not just of the hassle we'd get, although obviously coming out at school was fatal then, it still is now! But also, part of me really thought that it was wrong and bad. As if you can help who you fall in love with!' Colin looked over at Anthony, who looked back with a smile in his eyes. 'He was so much braver than me. I always wondered if, when he heard it, he knew it was him I was singing about.'

'But it turned out that a teenage girl thought it instead, seventeen years later,' Anthony said.

'I have to explain. This was my doing, all of it,' Harry said. 'I got very taken with the idea of playing detective and I think I've put Rain through a lot of unnecessary stress and disappointment. Rain, I'm really sorry. Colin, I'm really embarrassed. Anthony. I hope you can all forgive me.' Rain stared at Harry; he seemed very grown-up, all his usual playfulness gone completely. 'I think I'd like to go home and hit myself in the head. Rain, would you mind taking me?'

Colin Thurber gave the diary back to Rain. Rain stood up and held her hand out to Harry without thinking.

'It was nice to meet you both, anyway, honestly,' Anthony said. 'I hope you're okay, Rain. And I hope you find what you're looking for.' Colin seemed a little more thoughtful, but he walked them to the front door.

'I'm sorry I couldn't have helped you more,' Colin said. 'It's okay, you coming here. Honestly. I'm glad I could be definite about it for you. I was never the groupie type, but I'm sorry you still don't have the answers you wanted.' He leaned against the threshhold as if he needed the support for a moment. Rain felt intensely awkward – she'd come here half-expecting to meet her father, while to him she was just a strange girl off the street with a bag of nutty theories. Colin smiled kindly, pressing his lips together. 'It would have been sort of nice to have an instant daughter, Rain.'

'I don't know what to say,' Harry said, as they walked back to the Tube station, so quickly they were almost running together. 'I'm such an idiot. I really thought I'd . . . well, it doesn't matter what I thought.'

His voice seemed to be coming from somewhere else. Rain's ears were half-deafened by the rush of blood to her head. Her cheeks burned, she could feel her feet hitting the street in strange distant thuds, but it was like she wasn't making them walk, they were just moving, somehow keeping going when the rest of her was switching off. 'What am I doing?' she kept thinking over and over. 'Where are the people who keep me on the ground? How have I let myself get *here*, without anyone I trust looking out for me?' Harry was still talking, beside her. Rain wanted her dad, but she felt as though she'd betrayed him. Even if she didn't tell him, maybe he'd know, he'd sense it, and things would never be the same again. She wished she could get on a train and go home, real home, but her dad wouldn't be there. And she wanted him so much.

'Well, say *something*?' Harry said, and Rain realised she'd stopped listening to him. She breathed in and felt as though she couldn't make a sound even if she wanted to, as if her voice had been stamped down too deep inside her. '*Rain*.' Harry touched her forearm. His hand felt strange, a stranger's hand. 'I'm *sorry*,' he said.

'It's not your fault,' Rain said. She made sure he could see her face to make him believe her. She wanted him to believe her or she knew she'd shout and cry. 'It's *fine*. I brought my problem to you, you were trying to help me. You even wasted your Saturday night doing it, well, some of it. You've probably still got time for a drink with Madrigal, you can tell her how it went.'

He looked weirdly pale, and Rain was afraid he'd say something angry, although she didn't know what Harry had to be angry about. Then she started getting angry in response to Harry's anger, even though it hadn't happened. She could imagine shouting at him, 'WHAT THE HELL ARE *YOU* ANGRY ABOUT? You've let me make a complete idiot of myself and I'm still nowhere nearer to finding out what happened before I was born!' Harry walked next to her, a little in front, so she could see his jaw clenching and unclenching; but he didn't say a word, so Rain had nothing to shout at. The tension of the unshouted anger seemed to resonate around them, like echoes from an argument that had already happened.

The sun was setting and Camden seemed more alive than it had when it was light. A man with long tangly hair and a beard was sitting on the stairs leading to the Tube station playing bongo drums, and the galloping beat gave the evening a sultry, throbbing soundtrack. Rain felt electricity in the air, a sense of danger and excitement; she suddenly realised how *relieved* she felt that she hadn't found her father today. She hadn't had to accept anything new or talk to him and worry about never loving him or never knowing him. She'd escaped, and now at the end of today her own dad was still her dad. But her body was drained and couldn't hold all the emotion. She used up the last of her energy to walk faster, and take the lead.

'I'm not going to tell Madrigal what happened,' Harry said, quietly.

'Oh, I bet you're not,' Rain snapped, not even sure if she meant it sarcastically. Her voice resonated in her own ears: it sounded horrible.

'I didn't tell her . . . what I *thought* we were doing,'

Harry said. 'It's bad enough that I messed this up without you thinking I'm going to be talking about you in the pub or something.'

'So what did you tell her? You'd have to have had some reason for . . . '

'I said we'd been talking about the band and I was amazed you'd heard of them, and you said your best friend's mum was a Sandcastles fan and your friend had asked you if you could get an old album signed for her with a personal message for her mum's birthday.'

'Wow,' Rain said flatly. 'Good lie. If I can offer a critique . . . ' Harry held out his palm, inviting her to carry on. 'Well, I'd have to say it's over-complicated, and I'm not sure you should get credit for being able to lie to your girlfriend so easily, but on the other . . . '

'Madrigal's not my girlfriend . . . ' Harry said, tilting his head to one side to look at Rain.

Rain put her face down. She could tell it was red because she got pins and needles in her lips when that happened. She gave a mean little shrug.

'Rain, I'm sure you've realised I . . . '

Rain was still looking down and couldn't see Harry's face. She suddenly felt terrified all over, suddenly shyer than she'd ever felt before, and hopelessly, hotly sweaty. She had to get away from Harry. Anywhere. Now. She tried to keep her voice normal. 'It's time I went.'

'Let me take you home,' Harry said.

'I know where I'm going,' Rain said. 'There's no point you coming out of your way.'

'Don't be silly, Vivienne would never forgive me if I let you get the Tube alone. I'm not going to let you walk off at night on your own . . . '

'You know, but, Harry, the trouble is, I'm just really . . . still . . . *angry* about what happened today, and I need to not be around you.' Without looking back, Rain ran through the tunnel and hopped on to the train without checking it was the one she wanted. The closing door caught her shoulder, and all the doors on all the carriages sprang open again. The people in Rain's carriage who'd seen what she'd done tutted at her for causing a delay, but Rain was just very grateful that she and Harry didn't have to wait on opposite platforms looking at each other. She sat on the train with her legs neatly crossed at the ankles, not spending too much time looking at the other passengers in case they looked back at her. She tried to look relaxed and sassy, but she felt like a little girl travelling alone for the first time in her life.

From:	rain@zoctine.com
Subject:	Important, but please don't panic, everything okay
Date:	7 August 1.58 a.m.
To:	s.lindsay@zoctine.com

Dad, I would have given anything not to have to write this email, but I'm feeling desperate and for all of my life you've been the person who's made me feel loved and certain and I want to feel that again now. You know I've been having a great time at Gran's and I'm very happy, so don't cut your trip short or anything, I don't want you to come home.

But.

Dad, I found Mum's diaries from when she got pregnant with me and I've worked out a little about what happened then. It's scaring me and confusing me and I don't know how to be about it. I know it must be painful for you, but the thing is, I just need to know more, I need to know where I came from and how you and she found each other and

And I'm not going to send this email either, am I?

Rain deleted the email again.

Chapter 12

Rain had hardly slept. She'd been thinking everything over, trying to remember how she would have come across to Harry. Had she seemed ungrateful, or immature? Stroppy? Normal? What would be a normal way to act in that situation? She lay in the dark whispering some of the things she'd said to hear them again, wishing she could change what had been said. She'd tried not to look at the clock, which seemed to steal another hour's sleep every time she glanced at it.

But the same restlessness woke her early the next morning, her dry mouth and throat confirming that she had finally slept. The embarrassment was still pumping through her like blood. The thought of going round to a stranger's house and accusing him of being her father felt totally crazy today. She felt hot all over again with anger at Harry. He'd texted her by the time she'd got in, asking if he could call, but she hadn't texted back. It wasn't really that she couldn't speak to him. She just needed him to know how upset she was, how important it was. Beyond words upset. Beyond words important. They'd talk about it, of course, but not right now.

Her grandmother was still asleep. Rain tiptoed downstairs and switched on the telly, then sat on the sofa with her legs tucked underneath her. She found an old musical she'd seen a thousand times when she was younger, and watched it until she forgot about being herself.

By the time Vivienne had come downstairs, Rain was feeling less vulnerable, and could answer her granny's questions about the previous evening with an easy sequence of white lies. They'd been to the pictures, she told her gran, but the film they'd been planning to see had sold out, and the other two films were terrible, so they just had a cup of coffee in Camden and left. Yes, Harry had seen her home, although the Tube in the evening wasn't scary at all.

They heard Rain's mobile in the kitchen, bleeping to say she had a text. Rain put the kettle on as she checked it. Harry again.

'You have to ask Vivienne. That's who you have to ask.'

Rain started tapping in a reply, but she knew she just wanted to have arguments with Harry while he was safely somewhere else because . . . she craved it. She longed to do the thing where she talked and he talked and she talked again and they kept going with their eyes meeting. It was so moreish; she could happily spend hours doing it and never feel bored, even if they never said anything new. He was under her skin: but she had let him in too far. He knew too much about her and she knew almost nothing about him. This was no time to think about playing games with Harry. He was right to send her the text like that, not to offer help. Rain had to do it alone, and she had to put her phone away.

She'd been afraid to ask her gran, because she'd felt it would be cruel talking about Sarah's secrets to her, things Sarah might not have wanted her mum to know. It would be emphasising the distance between Sarah and Vivienne, rather than remembering their love and closeness. So Rain had kept quiet, even though they sometimes came close to discussing exactly those moments of Sarah's life, and Vivienne talked the usual line: the things Rain had always been told were true, as if there were no complications at all.

How much did Vivienne know? Did Sarah tell her the second she knew she was pregnant? Did they buy the test together and hold hands as they waited for the result? Or had Sarah been alone, terrified, wondering what the hell she'd tell her mum if the test was positive? Rain's gran was so lovely it seemed hard to believe that

Sarah hadn't been close to her: she was down-to-earth and modern and young, she would have understood, she would have been calm, she'd have been *perfect*. Or maybe she'd have reacted exactly like practically every other mother Rain knew.

Rain told her granny she fancied a walk and she'd get the Sunday papers and some croissants for their breakfast. At the weekend, Londoners seemed to get up later than people in her home town. The perfectly groomed fashionistas were nowhere to be seen, and Rain saw just a few hung-over-looking men in tracksuits and baseball caps. The sunshine was pearly, gentle, and fat flowers bulged over garden walls, filling Rain's head with the scents of geraniums and honeysuckles. The pressure of being in such a happy place, being so unhappy, got to her, and her eyes filled with tears. She passed by more tracksuited men and one of them glanced at her flushed face and shiny eyes and couldn't help staring, and now she couldn't hold the tears any longer. She cried properly, little whimpering sounds strangled in her throat. She felt herself getting dizzier as she tried to see through the tears, until she had to sit down on a wall outside a little church. It was in the middle of a council estate, one of the few places in the neighbourhood which wasn't surreally rich. Rain looked for a bit of her clothing to wipe her nose on and didn't find any, so she just rubbed her face with the back of her hand, until the crying stopped and her embarrassment started to outweigh her unhappiness.

'Are you all right, darlin'?'

Two boys on bikes, a year or two younger than her, but quite a bit taller, had stopped where she was sitting.

Rain looked up at them. She nodded, and then sniffed more loudly than she'd meant to; it seemed to echo in the quiet enclave. 'I'm okay. I'm just a bit emotional.'

'He's not worth it!' said the taller of the boys.

'We were saying, we think you're lovely,' said the other one. 'Ten out of ten.'

It didn't feel at all as though they were trying it on with her – they'd just decided some boy had broken her heart so they were trying to cheer her up.

'Thanks,' Rain croaked. The boys stayed with her a moment, and the three of them were quiet, with just the sounds of birds singing and one of the bike wheels ticking as it spun around.

'If you need any help getting where you're going, just let us know,' said the taller boy, and they tactfully withdrew to start kicking a little football around in the street. Rain watched them for five minutes, then she got up and waved to them as she set off. They waved back. 'He's not worth it!' repeated the taller boy. 'Don't even let him apologise. Don't have nothing to do with him!' and they laughed and Rain smiled. She made her way back to her gran's house. She checked her phone, but there were no new texts. She read Harry's last one again, but still didn't reply to it.

They were both full, with flaky, jammy dishes in the sink and the bits of advertising that fell out of newspapers and magazines scattered all over the floor, when Rain made her move.

'Gran, I need to ask you something very personal about my mum. It may be all new to you and it may be upsetting or . . . '

'What?' Vivienne said. She sounded worried, despite Rain's attempt to make her voice light.

Rain had been rehearsing what she'd say outside on her walk, but she was still tempted to slow it down as if the words were just coming to her and she was feeling her way through. That way she could back out and change her mind, run away. As it happened, she just went for it. Vivienne listened as Rain explained. What she'd read in Sarah's diary, what Harry had said, how her world had been tumbling in on itself since she saw those weird initials, and now she was reaching out, hoping her granny could help.

'Oh Rain,' Vivienne said. 'How could you?' Rain sighed, the breath pulled at her insides, all the way to her stomach. 'How could you go through all this alone and not tell me you were sad when I could have made you feel better in seconds.'

'So you know about this?' Rain said. Her head had started to feel light and lost; her hands felt heavier, cold and shaky. 'Who is my real father and how did my dad get involved?'

'There's no real father!' Vivienne said. 'Sarah called your dad Quentin because he was playing in a terrible band when she met him – it was just a silly sort of nickname that stuck for a while. She liked Lavender Sandcastles at the time. But not even that much, so the idea that she was Quentin Vienna's groupie is quite funny. For one thing, he's gay.' Rain looked incredulously at her. 'Oh, Rain, mothers always end up listening to the crap music their daughters listen to, of course I know about him.'

'Well I know he's gay *now*,' Rain said with a half-smile, carefully getting back to the point. 'I met his partner, Anthony.'

'Oh, how nice,' Vivienne said. 'Does he still seem like a famous person or . . . '

'Gran, are you telling the truth?' Rain was pretty shocked: she was trying to get to the bottom of her father's actual identity and Vivienne seemed more excited by the fact that she'd met Quentin Vienna. 'I mean, Dad was in a *band*? But he'd have told me something like that. I mean, he's never said anything about it, nothing even *like* that.' Rain couldn't keep the hurt out of her voice. She'd spent so much time with her dad, and here was a big thing she didn't know about him.

'It wasn't a proper band,' Vivienne said. 'He was just messing about for a few months in one as a favour to a friend. Someone dropped out, I think, and they asked him to fill in. They played a few pubs and maybe that was where Sarah met him. I swear to you, Rain! There's no mystery here. I'm afraid the truth is not very exciting because it's what you already know. I didn't know she called him Quentin in her diary, but she used to call him that to me, and I used to call him Quentin as well, until he started turning up at the house, and then very soon after that it was rather a tense time and for a long while no one was making many jokes at all.'

'You mean when she got pregnant.'

'Yes. I'm . . . I've always worried I wasn't a very good mum to her at the time. And I think, or I've always been convinced that's why your dad didn't bring you to see me so much after Sarah died. I'd hate to think he didn't feel comfortable with me even now, and it had stopped us being better friends.'

'Gran, how can any of that be true? You're super-hip, and this was seventeen years ago, you must have been so young.'

'I was young.' Vivienne leaned back and stared at the ceiling. She started to smooth back her hair with both hands. 'I was too young to be rational. I panicked.

Before it happened I thought I was incredibly cool and modern. I used to brag to everyone that Sarah and I were more like sisters than mother and daughter. And then my sixteen-year-old daughter came home pregnant. My perfect, clever girl with all her life in front of her and it felt like the end of the world. How *stupid*.' She leaned forward again and looked straight at her granddaughter. 'You were fabulous, from the moment you were born, Rain. We all loved you so much: your granddad, I'd never seen him smile the way he did when he first saw you. Your dad, my God! We all knew he'd do the right thing and be there for Sarah, but no one could have expected him to fall in love with you the way he did. He was smitten, absolutely mad about you. He made up songs, and rocked you in his arms and sang to you for hours in the middle of the night – you were all living with me, and I used to hear him getting up and then two minutes later his bloody stupid songs.' Vivienne closed her eyes and smiled the most beautifully relaxed smile. 'Sarah hadn't ruined anything – something lovely had happened.'

Rain had to hear it again. 'You're saying the QV in my mum's diary is *my* dad. My dad, Sam Lindsay.'

'Well duh, Rain, why would we lie to you?'

'But I've been worrying about this for weeks!'

'Why didn't you just ask me?'

'I thought you'd be upset. Or that you didn't know.

Look . . . there's no chance you didn't know and he's someone else?'

'RAIN! There's no chance! Let's find some pictures of your dad at the time and then let's find some pictures of you and see how much you look like your dad.' She went over to some deep drawers at the back of the room.

'Thank God I didn't ask my dad about it.'

Vivienne laughed. 'I think he'd think it was funny. I should tell him anyway.'

'Gran, don't. Please. It hasn't been funny at all.'

'Here.' Vivienne came back to Rain and handed her a little pile of photographs. Rain looked through them, feeling her hands getting a little trembly again.

'Oh . . . ' she said. 'It's Mum and Dad when they were teenagers! Why haven't I seen these before?'

'I don't know, you should have,' her granny said. 'They've usually been packed up or stashed away or something. But when I moved from Germany I found out where some of my more precious things were, so I can put my hands on them again. She was so lovely, wasn't she? Very like you. But you're like your dad, too.'

Rain gazed into the blurry little pictures: Sarah smiling shyly, her dad trying to look cool. He looked like Quentin Vienna. But he looked more like Rain.

'This isn't what you've been doing with Harry, is it?

173

I thought you two were doing scrummy romantic things around town, not reading old copies of *Smash Hits* looking for clues. If I'd known I'd have forced you to do more things with me. I didn't want to cramp your style.'

Feeling awkward again, Rain started turning the pages of a Sunday magazine. 'There's no . . . romance, Gran.'

'Oh, okay,' Vivienne said. 'Well it's a shame, because he's a good-looking kid.'

'Yeah,' Rain said quietly. There was nothing more to say. She didn't want to hurt her granny's feelings by being touchy. She read her horoscope at the back of the magazine. It talked about her career plans coming together this week.

'What a mess,' Vivienne said. 'I wish you'd trusted me.'

'It was nothing to do with not trusting you,' Rain said. 'It was about not . . . upsetting . . . things.' Her body was flimsy, still set up to hear life-changing things. It was like she'd been pushing hard against a door, trying to stop it opening towards her, then it had opened the other way, leaving her falling into nothing.

'I don't want *you* to feel bad, Rain,' Vivienne said.

'I don't feel . . . ' Rain said, but she didn't finish the sentence.

Rain's diary

7 August

I hate this feeling. The emptiness. It's almost as if I'd *wanted* Gran to tell me all about my real dad, like I'd wished there really was another story there. I feel guilty for not just simply being incredibly happy. I *am* happy, I am *incredibly* happy. But not simply. Before this, I've always had to live with never really knowing my mum. Now it turns out I've never really known my dad.

At the back of it all, the thing that feels good – or good isn't the word, what it feels is SAFE – is that my dad is my dad. The truth is, the real reason that mattered so much was that I was so scared of things changing, and so scared of losing him – HIM: Sam Lindsay – and, if he found out I wasn't who I was, there was always a chance he might not have wanted to be around me so much. But I never wanted to have to get to know the stranger who had had something to do with my birth but *nothing* to do with my life.

I tried to call Georgy, see if she could somehow pick up a signal, but it didn't happen, then I started writing her an email in case she'd taken a day trip out to somewhere with an internet café. But I binned the email and just came back to my diary because I couldn't find the right tone, there was too much to say, and I realised I needed to say it to my dad before anyone else. This is weird and wrong, but I'm sort of cross with my dad for the fact that I was fooled, for it all having been a surprise. I know that his life is his own, and he doesn't know everything I think, and the older I get the less I will tell him. That makes me sad. I don't have any right to expect him to have told me everything that's ever happened to him, that he met my mum when he was playing in a band, that she had a nickname for him, or any of it. But I feel like he should have tried harder to tell me about her. I know it must have been hard.

Also: I feel bad that I blew up at Harry. I was angry because he'd rushed us into doing something stupid and embarrassing, but that wasn't all, because that was okay, really, Quentin/Colin was nice about it and we're all still alive. It was . . . there was something happening, even before Harry said that Madrigal wasn't his girlfriend. I kept wanting to lean on him and touch him as if it was the most natural thing in the world, and then realising that I wasn't really supposed to do that, he hadn't given me any reason to think I could. It's not so much like he gets me or we're the same person, it's just like I want more of him, I want to know what he thinks about everything, and when I think something I want him to know what I think and to tell me something else. I find it hard to stop. But at the same time I'm scared, because Harry's not a kid and I don't want to seem like a kid and get it wrong. On Saturday night he seemed to come close to saying something about us, but I didn't let him because I wasn't in any state to hear it anyway, because of what had just happened. Then I was horrible, then I ignored him, and I'm left wondering if there's anywhere else for us to go . . .

I'm no good at this kind of thing. Harry is going to have to realise that and be good enough for the both of us, or it's not going to happen. Ha ha, I talk like I know he still wants it to happen! Is that possible? Or have I been stupid enough to put him off?

Chapter 13

On Monday morning, when Rain came downstairs for breakfast, she found her grandmother frowning, distractedly folding the edge of her newspaper into a concertina fan.

'Harry's not coming in today,' Vivienne said, looking up.

'He isn't?' Rain said. She was nervous, although she didn't know why. 'What did he say?'

Her granny peered at Rain a bit more intently than usual. 'He said he wasn't sure when he'd be able to come back, and that something had come up that he couldn't get out of.'

'Oh.' Rain felt cold inside. 'Does that mean . . . Madrigal's coming on her own?'

Vivienne's frown relaxed into a sudden smile. 'I'm going to go out on a limb and guess that's *not* going to happen,' she said. 'I suppose it must be a very last minute thing or Harry would have mentioned it to you on Saturday night. I hope he's okay.'

'Yeah,' Rain said, meekly.

'He didn't say anything, did he?'

'No,' Rain said, rounding her eyes.

'I don't really know what we're going to do without him.'

'Oh, I bet we do all right,' Rain said.

But they missed Harry. Madrigal, as Vivienne had predicted, didn't turn up either. Rain and her gran spent the day sanding doors to prepare them for varnishing, and they were both quickly exhausted and mostly silent. The work seemed harder without Harry's jokes and sweetly silly questions: making everyone rate each other in order of geekiness (Harry put Vivienne at the top and said she just hadn't realised what was out there for her yet) or asking them to name their favourite song that told a whole story (Rain's was 'Common People' by Pulp, because it was her dad's favourite song, Harry's was 'The Gambler' by Kenny Rogers).

By lunchtime they were hot and hungry, but Vivienne just made sweaty little cheese sandwiches, rather than sending Rain to the deli, which was what usually happened when Harry was around. After Rain and her gran had eaten the sandwiches, neither of them felt like starting work again, so Rain went to call her dad and

Vivienne lay on a sofa that was drenched with sunlight from the curtainless window, and immediately fell asleep.

Rain wasn't supposed to call her dad today: she knew he was on a field trip. He was halfway up a mountain when he answered his mobile. He was puffing like mad and the line was bad. He apologetically warned her he didn't really have time to talk. As soon as she heard his voice, Rain was almost drunk on the emotion, she got light-headed and tongue-tied. She felt how much she was missing him. She didn't have anything to say to him, because she had too much to say, and nothing at all that could be said over a phone to someone on a mountain. He tried to explain how beautiful the view was, while she pressed her phone hard into her head, trying to hear his near-breathless voice through the breaks in their connection.

She'd really believed she might have lost him, and he would never know.

Over supper, a takeaway pizza, Rain and her gran mutually agreed to abandon work on the house until Harry came back. But after calling Harry early next morning, Vivienne sat down at her computer and started writing another ad.

'What are you doing?' Rain said, looking over her shoulder.

'I just can't tell if Harry's going to come back,'

Vivienne said. 'He sounded weird today. He couldn't come up with a good reason not to come tomorrow, which is why I think he isn't going to come.'

'But that doesn't make any sense!'

'It does to me. Rain, did . . . ' Vivienne chewed her thumb. 'This isn't about you two, is it?'

'What do you mean?' Rain said, with over-played innocence.

'That's why I haven't pushed him harder about coming back,' Vivienne said. 'I'm afraid he's upset you, and he's staying away.'

'No, not at all!' Rain protested.

'Or the other possibility, of course . . . you upset him,' Vivienne said, comically biting her bottom lip. She smiled.

'Oh, Gran, come on.'

Vivienne had guessed her thoughts. The harder Rain tried to remember what happened when she and Harry met Quentin Vienna, the more it played out in her head as a kind of TV highlights package of her being impulsive and brattish. She'd made it very clear to him how angry she'd been and how much she'd blamed him. After that she'd just run home when he was trying to talk to her. If Harry had given up fixing Vivienne's house because he was trying to avoid facing Rain, it would be no surprise to her – or, it now turned out, to her granny.

Rain's diary

9 August

Well, that's it, then, I've totally messed up. Am I being completely egotistical thinking I'm the reason he hasn't come back? I mean, Gran said it, not me. But it must be me, because why hasn't he texted me? I mean, APART from the three texts he sent me the night we went to Colin's house, the texts I totally ignored because I wanted to make some kind of POINT.

Question: is he ignoring me because he thinks I don't want to hear from him, or is he ignoring me because after the way I've treated him he doesn't want to hear from me?

And is that it? Is he going to come back, and if he isn't, how do I persuade him to without . . . actually *talking* to him?

The summer is disappearing before my eyes like a wool jumper unravelling – what seemed like weeks and weeks, because I was missing Dad so much, now seems like no time at all. I keep thinking, if Harry comes back tomorrow, how many days do I have left to let him know what I feel about him? It's not enough days. And what if he doesn't come back at all?

Chapter 14

It was Friday when they came back – both Harry *and* Madrigal – with quick and vague apologies about Madrigal having family commitments ('Oh yeah?' Rain thought childishly, 'had to be there for Big Roy, did you?'), and Harry nodding but not saying much. Rain glanced his way for a millisecond, to find he was looking at her. She chanced further looks at him when she thought it was safe, but he didn't look back again. Rain made excuses and went out soon after they'd arrived. She caught the first bus that came and stayed on it, not sure of where to get off – maybe she'd just take it as far as it went and then worry about how to get back later.

She worried she was being childish, but she didn't know how else to be – the situation was really difficult, really embarrassing. They'd said nothing to each other since Harry had sent those texts that she hadn't answered. Rain looked out of the bus window. The first time she'd taken this route was with Harry, the day she'd been chased by a robot and they'd talked in that weird, tucked-away little pub. Then she'd taken it again with him when they went to the Tate Modern to see the Andy Warhol exhibition. Rain wished she could forgive Harry and Harry could forgive her without either of them actually having to have the conversation, but she'd taken it too far by ignoring him and he'd taken it too far by staying away, and now she didn't know how to get back to normal.

At St Paul's Cathedral, Rain got off the bus – it was nearly the last stop and she was the only person left on the top deck. She walked halfway across the bridge she'd crossed with Harry, the shiny silver Millennium bridge, and leaned hard on the rail, looking down the river. The sun reflected on the river was dazzling. Little kids on day-trip boats waved and called to the people on the bridge. Rain was in London, her mum and dad's home town, and London was brilliant. She closed her eyes and felt the breeze blowing her hair back, then she laughed gently, biting her bottom lip. It was time she stopped worrying and started remembering she was on holiday. And time to give Harry a break, too.

In the second bedroom on the first floor of Vivienne's house, Harry and Madrigal were taking a Madrigalinitiated break while Vivienne was out. They sat on the floor with their legs out straight in front of them, leaning on a dust-sheet covered sofa, drinking cans of Coke. Madrigal fiddled with the radio, turning the volume up.

'Ach, how many more weeks of this?' Madrigal said. 'It's our holidays, Harry, we are going to get a few weeks off at the end of it, aren't we?'

'Mads, you don't need the money, why are you even still here?' Harry said.

Madrigal shrugged, looking away from him. 'I thought you needed the help,' she said.

'The help's great,' Harry said. 'You know I'm grateful, it's just that I'm feeling guilty.'

'You don't have to. It's fun hanging out, isn't it?'

'Yeah,' Harry said, nodding enthusiastically. 'I've been having fun. Well, until I blew things with Rain.'

'Blew things?' Madrigal said. 'There were things, then?'

Harry almost jumped, as if it surprised him that he'd said too much. 'No. I just . . . well, it's not really something I can talk about, I just let her down, something I said I'd do for her.'

'What, that thing with the old muso friend of my dad's?' Madrigal said. 'You don't have to tell me.' Harry smiled, relieved. 'I'm sure I can find out from my dad,' she added.

'Ah, don't, Mads!'

Madrigal giggled. 'I'm just joking!' She reached into her pocket and took out a little sachet of loose tobacco. 'Open the windows, will you?'

'Vivienne'll know if you've been smoking,' Harry said.

'Possibly. Probably she won't care, though,' Madrigal said. 'She's quite a cool old lady. She knows what young sexy people get up to.' Harry obediently opened all the windows as wide as he could, and sat down next to Madrigal again, while she took a pre-rolled joint out of her tobacco packet, and lit it. She took a long drag, and then offered it to Harry. He shook his head. Madrigal exhaled. 'Come on, then, tell me what naughties you and the teenager have been getting up to?'

Harry smiled painfully. 'There's nothing.'

'But the old lady's been making you take her out.'

'Yeah.'

'And she's got a big Sandra Dee crush on you.'

'No, she . . . '

'And you're falling over yourself trying to hide that stupid crush you've got on her. It's not working, by the way, Harry.'

Harry let his mouth hang open, and it wasn't clear whether he was going to protest that it wasn't true or gapingly admire her powers of perception. He laughed stiffly, instead, and Madrigal took another puff and blew it approximately in the direction of the open window. She was smiling, but her eyes looked pink and restless. She started to sing along under her breath to a song on the radio.

'Vivienne'll be back soon,' Harry said.

'No, she won't,' Madrigal said. 'She's got to get all the way to the King's Road and back and she only ever takes buses – like you. It'll take her maybe two hours.'

'And she's already been gone an hour,' Harry said. 'Anyway, we should probably have something to show for the morning. Let's get back to it.'

'Well then, you start, Harry, I'm having a smoke.'

Harry moved his shoulders as if he was about to get up, but didn't. 'Mads, why *are* you here?' he said. His voice was low and his face was close to hers.

'Come on, Harry,' Madrigal said, not turning to face him. 'Am I the only person here who can spot obvious crushes?' She put her head down and stubbed out her joint on the top of her empty can of Coke, dropping the butt inside.

'Mads . . . '

'Harry,' Madrigal said, impatiently.

'You know how gorgeous you are.'

'Do *you*?' she said, finally looking at him. She gave him a little half-smile.

'You're way out of my league,' he said.

Madrigal's voice almost cracked as she replied. 'I'm not, you know.'

'Madrigal, you know you could get any bloke . . . '

'Look, I know,' Madrigal said, her voice stronger again now. 'It's Little Orphan Annie, you've got it bad for her.' She pushed her finger into the top of the Coke can, rasping it along the sharp edge. 'It's fine. Harry, how long have we known each other? If something was going to happen between us it would have happened. It's cool.'

'I'd better get back to . . . '

'Don't go yet.' She held his hand. He looked at her, his eyes warning and consoling. 'It's *cool*,' Madrigal said.

Vivienne, back from her trip to the King's Road, came upstairs with some cakes she'd just bought from the shop around the corner. When she reached the top of the stairs, she could see into the bedroom they were decorating today, and she could see Harry and Madrigal kissing. They didn't see her. She went back downstairs as quietly as she could.

'I can't do this,' Harry said, pulling back. 'I'm sorry, Mads, I didn't mean to make you think . . . '

'Oh, relax, I don't think anything,' Madrigal said. 'It's just the pot making me horny.' She leaned into him again. 'It's not like you're cheating on anyone. You said she doesn't want anything to do with you.'

Harry subtly held her away. 'She doesn't,' he said. 'I think she doesn't. But while there's a chance, I have to . . . and you know, even if there isn't a chance, I just can't think about anyone else right now. You said it, really. I've got it bad.'

'Well, I *told* you that,' Madrigal said, but there was no triumph in her voice. She peeled her clothes off his where they clung, and rolled away from him, taking a few steps on her knees. She fiddled with the radio again, rejecting every station and then turning it off. 'So you want to go out with a schoolgirl? That's your plan? A *northern* schoolgirl! They all get married at sixteen, you know.'

'That's not fair.' Harry tried not to sound angry, but he could hear the tightness in his voice.

'It was just a joke,' said Madrigal. 'She's the one, eh?'

'I have no idea,' Harry said. 'But when she's around, I can't think of anything, and when she's not around I can't think of anything else.'

'Oh . . . blah,' Madrigal said, and blew a fat, wet raspberry at him.

Rain was making her way back, walking through Trafalgar Square and past the National Gallery where

189

she'd gone with Harry to see *Boy Bitten By a Lizard*. She went inside, found the room with the Caravaggios and sat where she'd sat before, where her parents had sat together before her, and looked at the paintings. It was true what Colin Thurber had said – the diary didn't even name her dad's favourite painting, and she didn't know which one it was. She looked around, trying to guess. There was a quite intense one with the head of a beheaded John the Baptist on a plate, but that couldn't be anyone's favourite painting. The head was *green*. There was another with a beardless Jesus surrounded by people jumping up so quickly they went out of focus and almost out of the picture frame. She didn't know what made her so sure, but Rain was certain that it was the painting – something about it, she knew he'd love it. Rain realised that, even though she might not know much about his life before she was born, she knew him now, better than anyone.

In the gift shop, she bought the *Boy Bitten By a Lizard* postcard, and while she rode the bus home, tried to think of something funny but encouraging to write on it, to slip to Harry so they wouldn't *have* to talk or apologise. *Girl smitten by a Londoner?* Too much. She wrote: *From a girl bitten by London. Please don't be put off showing me more of the place because I had a bad day. Rain.*

* * *

190

Rain got back home a lot later than she'd expected to – after getting off the bus she'd wandered along the Portobello Road, dipping into the weird clothes shops, the Oxfam bookshop, and, last of all, stopping for the fabulous brownies Harry had bought her when she first went out with him. It was almost seven o'clock when she opened the door, and her gran was downstairs in the kitchen making paella.

'Hi, Rain,' Vivienne said, pushing her sleeves up further and wiping her hair off her face. 'You look . . . perky. Good day?'

'I had a fab day!' Rain said. 'It's lovely going places with people; but it's also good going it alone, actually, because you can spend exactly as long as you like wherever you want without worrying that you're boring the heck out of them.'

'And also you don't have to stay somewhere mind-numbingly boring because you're both waiting for the other person to say they've had enough. I agree.'

'That smells delicious.'

'It's nearly ready, if you wanted to eat right now, or it can just as easily sit?'

'I'm starving,' Rain said, and threw her shopping bags down, and came over to help her gran make a salad.

The paella was saffrony-fragrant, stuffed full of big langoustines. Rain ate two full bowls of it. Afterwards,

Vivienne was scooping ice-cream on to the brownies, which they'd warmed in the oven, and Rain tentatively asked how the day had gone in the house now that Harry and Madrigal were back.

'Oh. Right,' her gran said, and Rain stuck her elbows on the table, making fun because Vivienne's expression was quite serious. 'Well, I'm not sure how you'll feel about this,' Vivienne began, 'but it turned out I was wrong and you were right. By the looks of things, Madrigal and Harry *are* an item.'

Rain's stomach lurched as if she was in a lift that had just dropped unexpectedly. 'How do you know?' she finally asked.

'Oh, they were necking when I got home. They didn't see me, and I just left them to it – well, it was their break time.'

Rain couldn't think how to react, and Vivienne judged the silence correctly. 'Oh, sweetie, I'm sorry,' she said. 'I thought you were only flirting with him for fun.'

'Of course I was,' Rain said. She recovered quickly. 'It's just, you know, I feel funny now about going out alone with him if he's someone else's boyfriend. I don't think I'd like it if I had a boyfriend and he was going out with Madrigal. I suppose I don't seem like much of a threat to her.'

'Pah!' Vivienne said.

'Oh well,' Rain said.

'He's just not as smart as I thought he was,' Vivienne said.

'Stupid me for fancying someone so stupid,' Rain said.

The next morning it rained. A lot. Heavy showers lashed against the fragile old windows of Vivienne's house, streaming into the gutters in the street below. Vivienne stared out at her newly tidy garden; the smaller saplings the garden-clearance had uncovered were being bent backwards by the heavy rain, flower petals crushed flat.

Rain had gone for a walk.

The rain felt less nice than she'd expected. It slapped her face, got down her neck. She stood on a trick pavement slab that dipped four inches with her weight, spraying her leg with water and drenching her foot, so that the sock squelched inside her shoe. A lorry drove past, throwing up a wall of water that Rain tried to jump away from, but she was still splattered.

'Uch, I'm so THICK,' Rain said out loud, kicking an arch of water in front of her. She'd hoped to be spiritually cleansed by the rain, but she was just getting wet.

Rain was finding it hard to believe she'd been so wrong about Harry. Why would he have lied to her about Madrigal – was it all about tricking her into having sex? She laughed with embarrassment; if it was about him having sex with her he had seriously been taking his time – he hadn't even tried to kiss her. Then, horribly, she realised that her misunderstanding might have been almost the reverse of that – he hadn't ever been interested in her that way, he really could have been showing her around London just to be kind. In which case, the worst thing he'd done to her was tell her Madrigal wasn't his girlfriend, and he must have had some other reason for that – maybe she *hadn't* been his girlfriend then, and yesterday things had changed – they had, after all, been left alone for a day, without their boss and their boss's loopy granddaughter around. Well, lucky Harry.

She came home and shrugged comically at her gran's shocked expression on seeing how wet Rain was. Rain went upstairs to write an email to Georgina. It took her more than an hour: she included the whole complicated story about trying to trace her dad, all the way to how she ended up with Harry in the middle-aged gay couple's chic little house, but she found it a lot more difficult explaining what was happening with her and Harry right now.

Even my gran had been on at me to have a summer fling with him, and I swear to God he led me on! Do guys do

194

that when they're not interested? If they do, that's not fair! It seems to be breaking some kind of guy rule for them to pretend to be interested and not be interested in anything.

She was trying to be funny for Georgina, but she knew that what had happened between Harry and her was much more complicated. They had been *friends*. It hadn't just been wishful romantic thinking, it hadn't been imaginary. It had been a friendship that was much more natural and honest than any she'd had in her life – she felt completely herself with Harry – funnier and sillier and angrier and just BIGGER than she was with anyone else: she relaxed with him. However, she'd misinterpreted his boyfriend intentions, the friendship – the friendship – was real. She had to put her embarrassment aside (even though her instinct was just to hide, for ever) and stop sulking about losing someone who had never been hers.

Easier said than done when he had eyes like Harry.

Rain leaned her forehead against the cold window and looked out. It was still cloudy but brighter, and the heavy rain had almost stopped. The street below looked clean and peaceful and London felt small and manageable. Then Rain saw a walk she recognised coming round the corner, heading towards her gran's house: Harry was here.

Chapter 15

'It's Harry, Harry's outside,' Rain said to Vivienne, before he'd reached the house. She put on her shoes and coat – the shoes were freezing and soggy on her feet – and went out, shutting the door behind her. She pulled the cold damp coat tightly around her.

'Did you want Gran?' Rain said, but she knew he didn't.

'No,' Harry said.

'Shall we walk?'

'Yes.'

It was still lightly raining. They walked in silence until they were well past the end of the street.

'What did Vivienne say about things?' Harry said.

Rain was surprised he suspected that her gran might have talked about him snogging Madrigal. Then she realised he meant the mystery of her real father. 'Nothing. Everything's fine. My dad's my dad.

QV was code. It was nothing.'

'That's *it*?' He was shocked.

'Yes.'

'Wow.'

Rain could hear her shoes squelching. They didn't look at each other.

'How do you feel?' Harry said.

'Relieved?' Rain said.

'But not totally?' Harry said.

'No, yeah, relieved. But a bit abandoned too.'

'You know,' Harry said, 'I don't know anything about my parents as kids, or when they met, or the way they met. You could have shown me a . . . a Dickens novel or something and said it was my dad's diary and I wouldn't have thought it couldn't be. Well, except for the carriages instead of cars. Do you know what I mean? I don't think I put it very well.'

'But they talk about your brother, I bet.'

Harry rubbed his eyes with his palm. 'Yeah,' he said matter of factly. 'They do. But usually it's to say that I'm just like him, or I'm doing something he always did.'

'I suppose my dad talks like that, too.'

'So, maybe it isn't really for us, maybe it's to let themselves think there's still a little bit of the other person here with them,' Harry said.

'Yeah.'

'Are you going to tell your dad?'

Rain smiled. 'I'm going to practise telling him until I can tell it like a joke. I've already made a start on that, I keep running through it in my head, trying to make it funny. I thought I'd have Colin answer the door in one of his stage outfits.'

'I'm sorry,' Harry said. 'You know I'm really sorry about that.'

'I'm sorry I gave you a hard time, at the time. I'm fine about it now, you know. Really.' She shrugged.

'Are you disappointed you're not the bastard love-child of a one-hit-wonder . . . '

'Two-hit-wonder . . . '

' . . . the bastard love-child of a two-hit-wonder pop star?'

Rain laughed, and let her shoulder bump against Harry's, then wondered if she should have. Could you do that with a friend? But she was doing well, it was feeling normal again between them. She was being very grown-up and sensible. She wanted someone to congratulate her, because it might have helped her with the heavy pain of her bruised heart.

'So now what do we do?' Harry said.

'About what?' Rain said, feeling scared – had he found her out? Was he going to gently let her down by telling her about Madrigal?

'About me fancying you, dicking about every

moment of every day trying to impress you, thinking about you all the time?'

Rain's heart stopped beating, then started again with a big stumbling kick. 'Do you?' she said. She felt as if her face was very gently on fire, and she had to open her mouth to breathe.

'Yes. Do we do something about it, or do I . . . leave you alone?'

This was so strange: while there was nothing she'd wanted to hear more than this, the fact that she knew what had happened the day before made it worse than anything else he could have said.

'My granny said you were kissing Madrigal when she came in yesterday.' She began hesitantly and finished quite fiercely.

'Oh.' He made a small 'huh' sound, looking up at the still grey sky. It was enough to confirm it – she'd still stupidly been hoping her granny was wrong and he'd been trying to take a piece of grit out of Madrigal's eye or . . . a piece of grit out of her mouth . . . with his lips . . .

'I'm just having trouble working out how that would fit into your *constant* efforts to impress me, and . . . '

Harry didn't say anything. He was still sighing quite loudly.

'Well, you're not trying to deny it, anyway,' Rain said. 'I suppose that's something.' She looked up at him.

'I would have really liked you to try to deny it,' she said. 'I still want you to.'

'I can't,' Harry said. 'It did happen. You know, for . . . *ten seconds* I wanted to be kissed. Because I'd lost you. I'd ruined your life and made you sad and there was no coming back from that.'

'But you came back today.'

'Yeah.' He dragged his hand through his hair. 'As soon as she started kissing me I knew it wasn't what I wanted at all.'

'But why not?' she said. 'I mean, why would you not . . . she's completely beautiful, you obviously get on . . . '

'Right, I would *like* to pretend to be offended by that, and point out that men aren't completely stupefied by beautiful girls, but what with you looking like you do, I think people would laugh at me.'

'Oh, come on, I . . . '

'Madrigal's not my type. And she's funny, but she's *not that nice*. I quite like that in a friend, though. Everyone wants a friend who's a little bit bad.'

Rain pulled her frizzy, still-damp hair in front of her face. 'It still hurts, Harry.'

'Does it?' Harry said. 'I can't think of a way of saying this that doesn't sound terrible, but that makes me kind of happy, because maybe it means you . . . ? Rain, you believe me, don't you? How do you feel?'

They had reached the entrance to Kensington

Gardens now, and fell back into silence. The rain had stopped, but the park seemed deserted. The Peter Pan playground was empty. There was no one sitting on the benches. There was no one anywhere. Rain felt the pressure to make something happen – she knew she could kiss Harry here, now, everything was set up to make it right. She could . . . she could stand on her tiptoes and hold his shoulders. Or she could turn his face towards hers and . . . The thing was, Rain could think about kissing him, but she couldn't make it happen, she couldn't feel her way to making it natural. As they walked further through the park, Rain started to see more and more people. There were dog owners walking their dogs, some Japanese tourists under umbrellas, small groups huddled beneath the shelters in the café. A light breeze rustled the tall, old trees and rippled the duck pond, the geese and swans shaking their feathers out: the park was coming to life again.

And Rain knew she hadn't answered Harry's question.

'Maybe we should go somewhere warmer,' Rain said. Her feet were starting to hurt where the wet leather was rubbing them.

'Sorry, you look really cold,' Harry said. 'Come on, let's double back and get you somewhere warm.'

As they walked to a café, Harry made funny jokes about the people who walked past them, pointing out which obscure celebrities they looked a bit like, asking Rain to explain their strange behaviour and guess their names, and she enjoyed coming up with mad reasons, and she and Harry were just like they always were together. He'd given her the chance to ignore what he'd said, and while she waited for him to bring their coffees, taking off the wet shoes and rubbing her freezing feet, she considered taking it. He turned round to look at her from the counter, his floppy dark hair, flattened by the rain, in his eyes, the little half-smile checking that things were okay.

'I wish I could say something that would make me seem like a better guy,' Harry said. 'I was stupidly slow to catch on with Madrigal, which means I've been shitty to her, and I've screwed everything up. But the way I've felt hasn't changed since you walked into your grandmother's kitchen that first day.' He slowed down until he'd stopped speaking and asked her with his eyes, and Rain still didn't know what to say.

'I feel like we missed our moment,' she half-whispered.

'We missed it, did we?' Harry nodded and picked up a teaspoon, turning it over a few times. 'Oh.'

'I mean, there'd have been some moment where we just . . . kissed or something, in a fun way, and no one had to analyse it or worry about it because by then we wouldn't have . . . '

'What wouldn't we have?'

'But Madrigal was always in my mind, the fact that you weren't free to go around kissing people, so we didn't kiss then and we can't kiss now because . . . '

'Rain?'

Rain was speaking so quickly now she didn't know if she was making sense or not. 'Because now it's all changed and now I can't just be your holiday fling and you can't just be mine. And you *have* screwed things up. And there are consequences, and there are homes to go to, and there are times when everything is right but the timing is wrong, which is why I'm telling you we missed our . . . '

Harry leaned over the table and held Rain's cheek in his palm, and kissed her. It was a soft kiss, slow and steady, his hand moving back to the nape of her neck, gently holding her hair, and Rain felt so dizzy that she suddenly opened her eyes with a start, gasping and staring at him with her mouth still open.

'That's a pity,' Harry said.

'Well, it *is* a pity,' Rain agreed. 'And now no matter how much time we spend together the rest of the summer, and let me get this straight right now, we really should spend *every* minute of the rest of the summer together, I think we're just never going to get that —'

Harry kissed her again, and Rain carried on speaking into his lips for a second or two, then let her head spin away again, the way it seemed to when Harry was kissing her. On the other side of the kiss, she met his dark eyes again.

'Harry, I'm serious, though. I like you too much. I can't do this. You're at university, I'm at school. There has to be an end, and it's not all that far away. And it's going to *hurt*. I'm going to get upset and miss you.'

'We'll work it out,' Harry said.

PART THREE

Chapter 14

Rain was sick of seeing people in sombreros. They came past in groups of six or so, usually carrying tired-looking kids. The parents looked strained from trying to keep their holiday spirit intact all the way home, but also relieved to be back. Rain could remember that feeling, the first sight of British things after a foreign holiday – how everything seemed ugly and boring but, at the same time, comforting. She'd been at the airport since before ten o'clock, her dad's plane had been due just after ten-thirty and had landed about half an hour late. It was now well after midday, though she was trying not to look at her watch again because the hands didn't seem to be moving. For the first hour, she'd smiled constantly, the happiness inside her spilling out unconsciously. Now she wondered if she'd be so tired of waiting that she'd only give her dad a so-so welcome.

She needn't have worried. When Sam Lindsay's

long, thin, untidy frame came around the corner, Rain shouted 'Dad!' in a voice that was meant to be a decently audible call, but came out as a slightly deranged, very childish yelp. And her dad ran to her, scooping her into his arms and hugging her and hugging her, their heads together, tears in both their eyes.

'I've missed you so much, Rainy,' her dad said. 'God, you look so much older!'

'You look younger,' Rain said, laughing.

'So tell me what you've been up to,' Sam Lindsay said.

Rain's diary

21 August

Ack, I'm just like my mum, I never keep up with my diary when the things I'll want to read about are actually happening. I've probably forgotten things, well, not *forgotten*, but my head is now so full of things I need to talk about and my fingers won't go fast enough.

I felt a bit like that yesterday, just *talking*, when I wanted to tell my dad what my summer had really been like and I was tripping over my words, trying to dance around the bits where I'd have had to tell him I thought my mum had been in love with someone else when he first went out with her.

In the end I just told him. I hoped he'd laugh.

He didn't.

He said, 'I can't believe I've told you nothing about your mum, I can't believe you let me get away with that. I feel horrible. She was your mum and I owed you that. I owed *her* that.'

I said, 'But Dad, you've told me so much about her, you've told me loads of good stories and talked about how lovely she was. Besides, I *knew her* and I loved her.'

'Yes, of course, I'm sorry Rainy. But I never talked about her and me in the early days, how we met, the way I really saw her – not as your mum but as my girl. To not talk to you about that was almost like lying. You know why I didn't though, don't you?'

'Well, I thought it was because it would have been too . . . upsetting for you.'

'Yes.'

'So, Dad, you don't have to.'

Dad gave a little laugh. 'Well, you've read the diaries now, eh? You probably remember better than me.'

'Probably not.'

'No, probably not,' he said, smiling. 'So, where should I start?'

'It's not really where,' I said. 'More like when. So maybe not now, this minute, but tell me when it occurs to you, you know, when it's natural – just don't *not* tell me again?'

We ordered a Chinese takeaway – a break from our

usual rotation: Sundays traditionally being fend-for-yourself days. I'd eaten a lot of fancy food at Gran's, some of it successful, some of it a bit strange, and when our beef in black bean sauce and kung po chicken came, it tasted great. Then I made my dad talk to me about the early days, the Sarah's Diary days, hanging out with my mum – despite having just told him he didn't have to. I made jasmine tea to go with the takeaway, and we both drank tons of it and got giggly, the way you can on a lot of jasmine tea. For once, I didn't have any of that feeling of Sunday dread. Maybe I was just high on happy because I was seeing my dad again.

But a pot of tea later, Dad admitted he'd been in a band for a very short time – they were called The Strands – and I asked him why he never mentioned it or did anything musicky now.

'I was the singer,' Dad said. 'You know, you'd have known about it if I was one of those sad old dads bringing out a guitar all the time, but it's not the same for singers. I wasn't a good singer, either, I was just the frontman because I had the front.'

I looked at my sweet, geeky dad and wanted to laugh, but I didn't. 'So have you really not got any pictures of you lot playing?' I said.

'There were some taken at the time, but they just got lost,' he said. 'You move, you pack stuff up, different things get left in different places.'

This was when I got him to go and look for early pictures of my mum and him anyway, pictures I'd seen tons of times before. I needed to look at them together and know for sure that they'd been in love. I mean, I knew that everything Harry and I had been looking for had been nonsense, but there were a couple of reasons I needed a fresh look. First, it had never occurred to me before this summer that my parents hadn't loved each other *perfectly*, like people in films. But because that assumption had been shaken, even if it was just for a few weeks, I just wanted to . . . you know, sort of set my heart back on track, get all my senses back on board thinking that again. Second reason: I have never been in love before, and I needed to look at their love through my new loved-up eyes, as someone who knows. Because I knew that I would understand it all now in a way I never had as a kid.

I cleared the leftovers away while Dad went to look. He was gone ages. Eventually I went up to see what he was doing. I found him sitting on the floor in the middle of his office with pictures all round him, smiling. I picked some of the pictures up.

'Dad, I haven't seen these before,' I said.

'I know, I had a brainstorm,' he said. 'It suddenly occurred to me that there might be something in my uni files. But I haven't opened these boxes in a thousand years and there was all sorts of stuff I just . . .

forgot about.' Dad looked up at me with this really . . . *weird* smile on his face. 'Here,' he said, showing me a picture of some teenagers on stage. He was the one at the front, pulling a scary screaming face as he strangled a microphone stand.

'Dad, it's The Strands!' I said, feeling my whole head smile. I sat down on the floor with him, and held the picture. I never wanted to stop looking at it. 'What were you, *punks*?' I said, enjoying the taste of a word I think I might never have said out loud before. 'And is that *eyeliner*?' I looked round to see that he wasn't really listening: he was staring at a creased old sealed envelope.

'There's this, too, Rain.'

He turned the front round to show me. It said: *Rain, when she's old enough*. It was my mum's handwriting.

'What's that?' I said. I couldn't hear any more. My heart was going so fast and it was as if there was a big whooshing breeze right through the middle of my head, upwards, the edges of my vision sort of sparkled with little yellow stars. I was . . . *fainting*. But I didn't quite faint, I kept my eyes on my dad's eyes and tried to keep my breathing normal as he told me.

'Sarah wrote it. Not long after you were born. I can't remember when, a day, a week, I'm really trying to remember . . . She . . . she said she'd give it to you when you were her age – the age she was then – so you'd know how she felt when she, er, when you were born. She gave it to me because she always lost things and she said she knew I'd remember. I might have, but I stopped looking at these old things because, you know.'

'What does it say?' I said.

'I don't know. And quite honestly, I think I should read it before giving it to you because I *genuinely* don't know, not at all. But it's not addressed to me, is it?' He handed me the letter, and I saw his hand shake.

Dear Baby Girl

As I write this, we haven't even decided what to call you. I'm trying to decide between Rain and Patience, but your dad thinks we should go for something more 'normal'. I don't want normal. You're too amazing. I'm feeling so much for you that I need to share it with you, I have to set it down on paper, for keeps. I want you one day to know how I feel today.

But first I have a confession, and I need to get it out so I'm writing it here. You were not planned, and for a lot of the pregnancy I wasn't sure I was doing the right thing, my tiny little girl. In fact, I was sure I was doing the wrong thing. I used to lie with my head on your dad's lap while he stroked my massive stomach, and I'd say, 'What are we doing? I don't like babies! We've ruined our lives! We will never smile

213

again. We will never be the same again!' I said this . . . like EVERY DAY. Now let me tell you the truth: since you were born I haven't stopped smiling. I can't believe I get to keep you. I get to take you home. I get to hold you EVERY DAY. I can't stop staring at you. I told Sam we'd never be the same again, and I was right, and it's better than we could ever have hoped.

I have great plans for us. You, me and your dad. We'll see Africa together, and Rome and Brazil and Hawaii – well, if we ever have any money. We'll sing Christmas carols round the piano at Christmas. (We'll get a piano when we can afford one.) And money or no money, I promise you this: you will always wear fabulous shoes. I'm going to teach you everything I know about boys, and girls, and LIFE, everything you'll need to know, and you will be formidable and fearless and kind.

So you may not have been planned, little baby, but I can promise you that you are loved. Beloved. I have to stop writing now, because I can't stand holding a pen and paper when I could be holding you.

Love Mummy

Chapter 15

Rain's diary

7 September

I never saw Rome and Africa and Brazil and Hawaii
with my mum and I may never see them with my dad.
But who can say what'll happen? I didn't expect my
dad to fall in love again in Norway, for instance, but he
did. I approve; her name is Tibby, and she came to stay
last week. I didn't know how I was going to feel. I spent
the week before she came on the edge of crying all the
time. I couldn't understand why: I couldn't trace back
the tears to any one emotion I felt outright, so maybe it
was a mix of a lot of 'predictable' feelings – that it
somehow closed the book on his love for my mum –
that it was the end of our life together with just us, me
and my dad – that I knew that life had to end sooner or
later anyway – that I was afraid of someone new who I

haven't chosen coming all this way into my life – and that I was really, really happy for my dad. And then I met Tibby, and she was just like him, all absent-minded science-boffiny, but with nice hair, and all those abstract feelings went away, because she was real and there, and she's lovely. I love how light Dad seems around her: for so long before her he seemed to want to fast forward every day.

When Harry met Georgy . . . we were actually still in London. Georgy was allowed to escape from her family holiday a few days early and took the train (and the ferry, and maybe a little rowing boat rowed by a kindly highlander) straight down to see me. She spent the whole time shouting about her Scottish relatives and how she'd had to spend half the summer walking around lochs fighting off 'the midgies'. She pulled her hair back to show us both the bites. Harry didn't get a word in for the entire first day. But Georgy loved Harry, and Harry . . . was very entertained by Georgy. She was also quite impatient when she heard about our wobbly getting together and seemed to think she would have done away with all the insanity if she'd been around.

But coming home again felt like more of a culture shock than going to London had been. I went to a few parties with Georgy as soon as I got back and realised I'd sort of lost the knack of being me. Everyone seemed older, weirdly – I mean, they were, obviously, but older than *me* all of a sudden. I think I missed a really good summer, but I wouldn't have lost a minute of London, if I'd had the chance to choose again.

Now we're all back at school, it doesn't feel anything like going back used to. Instead of feeling like the year's going to go on for ever, it's more like we've got no time left at all. It's as though the shift to everyone thinking about university and their own lives has already happened, and the months ahead are nothing more than preparation for that. The people who are going out with each other are talking about how they'll cope. We're talking about where we'll *live*! I don't think I've changed, but at the same time I feel like my focus isn't on school any more. I don't worry about the things that used to obsess me, like making a fool of myself or keeping up with who's supposed to have fallen out with who this week. Like everyone else, I'm counting the days.

Gran and Harry are *both* coming up for my dad's birthday party. My dad has already bought himself a present: a guitar. He says he wants to show me how good he used to be and play me 'some old Strands licks', but when I hear him practising, it doesn't sound much like anything. He claims he's a bit rusty.

Harry's been up here quite a lot, at least every other weekend. He's also helping Gran move all her furniture downstairs into the rooms he – and Madrigal! – redecorated. Gran's not moving now: she's selling the upper floors, and staying in the ground floor and basement. A property developer came round and told her how much she could get for half the house if she split the place into two flats, and that was the end of her debt worries. I'm really pleased because I knew she didn't want to move; she likes it round there. She likes the market and the park, and the new shop that sells cupcakes just round the corner from her place.

So everyone's more together than ever, and it turns out my heart works fine after all because it gets very worked up when Harry's around. But it's just about when I'm happiest that I start aching all through my bones and thinking about my mother – Sarah – who has been around this summer more than at any other time since she died. Those things I remember about her, and the girl whose diaries I read, don't really fit together, because little girls never think of their mums that way. And older girls still have trouble getting their heads around it – the idea that their mother was once as unsure and silly and romantic and normal as them. If they're very, very lucky, she still is.

Also by Kate le Vann

Tessa In Love

Tessa has always been 'the quiet one', but when she falls in love for the first time, everything changes. Tessa finds a soulmate in Wolfie, a committed green activist, and she begins to look at the world very differently . . .

ISBN: 978 1 84812 000 6

Things I Know About Love

Livia's experience of love has been disappointing, to say the least. But after years of illness, she's off to spend the summer with her brother in America. She's making up for lost time – and then meets Adam. Can Livia put the past behind her and risk falling in love again?

ISBN: 978 1 85340 999 8

Two Friends, One Summer

Best friends Samantha and Rachel are spending the holidays with two families in France. As new experiences and boys threaten the trust between them, it looks unlikely that their lifelong friendship can survive this turbulent summer . . .

ISBN: 978 1 84812 001 3